FLOWERSHOP ASSASSINS

Bye Baby
So Pathetic
Raging Ranger

SO PATHETIC
Louise Collins
Copyright © 2022
Cover Design: https://www.booksandmoods.com/
Edited by: https://www.karenmeeusediting.com/

CHAPTER ONE

"I want a boyfriend."

The wail of a dying man would've brought Yates more joy. Ranger's self-pity routine had started to grate on his nerves. Every Friday night, he trundled off on a date with the enthusiasm of a horny cocker spaniel only to crawl into the flower shop the next morning like a dog on its last legs.

Yates ground his teeth. "Go get one."

"I'm trying. Every dating app you can think of, I'm on it, and nothing. It's dick pics, ab pics, feet pics."

"Feet?"

"I've been told my feet are cute."

Yates scrunched his face up and dropped his gaze to Ranger's boots.

"Hey, hey, can't have you getting a raging hard-on."

"Unlikely. Feet don't do it for me."

"Why can't it be like in the movies?" Ranger sighed.

"The movies?"

"A heated look with a passenger on a train. A grounded flight and only one bed at the hotel. A doomed ship that pushes two unlikely lovers together."

"You've got to stop watching Netflix alone. Blood, gore, and action. Those are the type of programs you should be watching."

"That's everyday life. I don't want to go home and see my everyday life. I want to see romance. I want to see a 'Will you marry me?' etched in the tag of a new puppy or a proposal with a Haribo ring at the airport."

Yates tossed his head back and cursed at the ceiling. "Sometimes I miss the old Ranger."

"Come on, you must feel something here." Ranger slapped his hand over his heart. "You're not made of stone."

"No, I'm made of blood, flesh, bone. All the stuff I hope to see flying through the air in a Netflix movie."

"You don't want a boyfriend?"

"Definitely not."

"Why not?"

"It'd involve giving a shit."

"Caring, you mean?"

"Look, I care. I care about the guy I'm screwing. I want him to enjoy it. I want him to leave feeling satisfied, but that's it. Emotions don't need to be involved."

"They don't need to be, but I *want* them to be. The way Donnie speaks about Elliot…"

"He called him a little shit the last time I spoke to him."

"Yeah, but it's how he says it. His tone. The affection. The fondness. The love in the way he says it." He sighed. "Little shit."

Sunglasses hid Ranger's eyes, but Yates suspected they were unfocused, welling up slightly.

He grunted. "You're thirty seconds away from getting thrown through the window."

Ranger took off his sunglasses and hooked them over the top of his vest. Just like Yates had predicted, Ranger's eyes were wide and shimmering. Back to the puppy dog look.

"I mean, what's wrong with me?"

He still wore his trademark black vest and mirrored shades, but he'd grown out the shaved part of his head with the tattooed snake. Not everyone liked snakes. Yates found his head boring to look at without the scar and the ink. Light-brown hair like most of the population.

"I think I'd make a good boyfriend."

"You kill people for a living."

"Does that make me a bad person?"

Yates folded his arms and levelled him with a glare. "It certainly doesn't make you Jesus."

"Fuck, Jesus…" Ranger pulled a red rose from a bouquet, and Yates flexed his biceps, flashing Ranger a macho display. *Put down my flower*. Ranger was too far gone to notice. He sighed as he spoke to the rose. "I would, you know?"

"Would what?"

"Fuck Jesus, that's how desperate I am."

"Pay someone to suck your dick and be done with it."

Ranger began plucking the petals away, dropping them to the floor. Yates nearly hyperventilated behind the counter, paralyzed by the sheer ludicrousness of Ranger's actions. That rose was from the premium bouquet. The biggest fucking roses in the county, and Ranger was sprinkling the petals from his fingertips.

"I know that's what you spend your money on, but I don't."

"And what do you spend yours on?"

"Magazine subscriptions and hopeless dates."

Yates lifted his eyebrow. "And we can see which of us is happier..."

"I don't want to pay someone. I know you like the no-strings sex scene, but I want the strings, and the fights, and the plates left in the sink, and the bins that need taking out. I want the drama."

He flung the stem away with a huff and reached for another rose.

"There will be drama if you pick up another."

Ranger rolled his eyes. "Domestic drama."

The bell to the shop sounded, and Yates plastered on his game face. A welcoming smile. He'd become a master at them. No hint of an assassin. Just a friendly flower shop owner that happened to be heavily scarred and tattooed and had impeccable taste in clothing.

His smile wasn't returned. The man who'd just entered locked gazes with Yates and didn't venture any further inside. He'd frozen, and in the odd stand-off, he paled.

"Hey..." Ranger whispered. Yates threw a sideways glance his way. "You might want to put down the guns."

"What?"

Oh.

Yates stopped tensing his arms and rested them casually on the counter. He smiled again. "Can I help you at all?"

The man strolled forward, seemingly at ease now Yates had stopped his threatening display of muscles. He came to a stop at the counter and held out his hand to Yates.

"I'm Adam. My girlfriend sent me."

He shook it, frowning at such a formal introduction.

"Lucky you," Ranger sighed.

Adam inched away from Ranger, who'd picked out another premium rose. Yates kept hold of his anger, but the smile he forced his lips into began to twitch.

"Ignore him. What was your girlfriend after?"

Adam shook his head. "No, *she* didn't want flowers."

Then why come into a flower shop? Yates bit his tongue and waited for an explanation. Ranger had begun picking petals again, taking Yates to boiling point. Sweat itched his scalp, and he used his sleeve to dab his forehead, but it didn't cool the anger drip feeding into his veins. Ranger was halfway through another goddamn rose, humming a cheerful tune under his breath.

Motherfucker.

"It's about Edna Green."

Yates blinked. The anger washed away. "Edna. Is she...?"

"No, she's still alive."

Edna Green. Seventy-years old. Grey, wiry hair. Could drive but really shouldn't. Lived on Maple Avenue with her cat Mr Big. Yoga on Mondays, bingo on Fridays, and had her weekly grocery shopping delivered on Saturdays. Terminally ill but determined to be active until her dying breath. She'd started coming to the shop months ago and sat staring at the flowers for hours, never bought any, though.

Ranger's fake cough pulled Yates from his thoughts. He blinked, focusing on Adam, who was looking edgy once again. He'd backed away from the counter. Yates's empty stare did wonders, but it wasn't the time to intimidate. It was time to listen.

"My girlfriend, Sandy, Edna's her grandmother, asked me to drop by before work. Edna's been coming in here a lot the last few months; she always comments on your shirts when we see her."

Yates looked down at himself. A particularly flowery number. Huge printed sunflowers, to be exact. Ranger's knee-jerk reaction upon seeing it was to burst out laughing. Then his tragic love life morphed it into an ugly sob.

"What does she say about them?"

"They're shit," Ranger muttered.

Yates gritted his teeth. His patience vanished. "Spit it out. What's happened to Edna?"

"She had a bad fall. She's fractured her pelvis. It's pretty nasty, and she could do with some cheering up. This is her favorite place to look at flowers."

That made Yates feel a surge of pride. There was nothing better than loyal customers. Except Edna had never actually bought anything. He smiled, and Adam smiled back. Everything was just peachy. Even Ranger destroying a rose didn't seem quite so infuriating.

"I mean, I wanted to go to the supermarket; they're half the price."

Yates dropped his smile. *Did this man want to die?*

"But Edna insisted the best flowers were here. So here I am." Adam reached into his back pocket and pulled out his wallet. "About to pay a fortune for something I could pull from the ground myself."

"No, you're not."

Adam glanced up with a sparkle in his eyes. "You'll discount them?"

So that was his game.

Yates smirked. "No, no discount. You can go get your supermarket cheap bouquet."

And preferably shove them up your arse.

"But—"

"I'll visit Edna with my own bunch."

Adam slipped his wallet back into his pocket, frowning fiercely as if he was genuinely perplexed. "Okay, but could you write a card saying they're from Sandy and me too?"

Yates lowered his gaze to the edge of the counter. The message Donnie had written in bold black marker pen screamed at him. He took a deep breath and looked at Adam, flexing his eyebrows.

"Get the fuck out of my shop."

Adam recoiled as if Yates had flicked him. Only flicked. If Yates had punched him, he would've gone sailing through the window. He laughed at his thoughts, a common occurrence since the shop had been petrol bombed and he'd hit his head diving through a window.

"I don't want any trouble," Adam murmured, retreating down the aisle.

Manic chuckling scared people. Sometimes Yates forgot. He tensed his arms, showing off his muscle and stared Adam down. A hit of satisfaction inflated his chest when Adam tripped while retreating.

"Don't come in here and insult my flowers."

Ranger threw a handful of red petals into the air like confetti. "Boy, is this bitch grumpy about his flowers."

Adam flung open the door and launched himself down the street. Yates ran his fingers over the message Donnie had stained his refurbished shop with.

DON'T ATTACK THE CUSTOMERS

"It's hard sometimes," Yates mumbled.

"Nil points for customer service."

Yates glared Ranger's way.

"He said supermarket bought are better."

"He said cheaper."

"My flowers are the best in the county."

Ranger sighed. "Since when was it ever about the flowers?"

"Since I won that award."

Yates gestured to the glass award on the side. The plaque read Best Bouquets and had a rose, much like the third one Ranger was destroying, etched into the glass.

The award was real. No intimidation, deals, or bribes. He'd won the award fair and square. His rose arrangements were fucking award winning, and Ranger had picked apart three from his goddamn premium bouquet.

"You're paying for those."

Ranger looked down at the petals covering the floor. "I'll tell you what, I'll buy some roses from the supermarket to replace the ones I took. No one will notice."

"Get out of my shop before I throw you out."

"Okay, okay," Ranger said, backing up to the door. "Later, bitches."

Yates tilted his head, glaring at Ranger until he registered his mistake.

"Fine, 'Later, bitch.' Is that better?"

"Just call me by my name."

"Got it. Later, bitch." Ranger slipped out of the door, flicked Yates the bird through the window, and disappeared up the street.

Yates took a long, hard look at his award, then disappeared into the back to attend other business. The windowless office reeked of damp, no matter what air freshener he tried. The two odors merged into a taste that clung to the back of his throat.

He could only endure the office for ten minutes at a time, but his emails confirmed there was no news on his elusive target. Mr Stevenson. It was rare Yates looked forward to a job, but Mr Stevenson was an interesting case. Child trafficker. One of the lucky ones that had escaped and managed to have a life afterward had hired Yates to kill him.

"Bastard," Yates hissed, checking his phone instead.

No messages, except Darius confirming they were still on that night. Yates flopped back in his chair. A night of fucking until they passed out. No strings. Yates liked to be dominant. Darius got off on being dominated. A sexual match made in heaven, and he'd got a new toy to try. Yates's cock hardened just thinking about it. He shoved it with a curse. He wasn't jerking off in the office *again,* no matter how tempting.

"Fuck, I'm sorry."

Yates jolted, stopped palming his cock, and swung his head towards the doorway at the foul-mouthed intruder. The man staring at him was young, slim, clutching his rucksack like his life depended on it.

His eyes were close to popping from his head.

"What the hell are you doing back here?"

He flinched and hugged his rucksack tighter. "I was here for…"

Flowers. *Of course.* Yates pulled himself together. He wasn't sitting inside his personal jerk-off space; this was the office to the flower shop. The guy was clearly after flowers, and instead, he'd got an eyeful of Yates's hard-on. He hadn't retreated, though. He shook like a leaf, his eyes shiny as if he was seconds away from tears. The sight of a clothed erection surely wasn't that traumatic, but color drained from his face until Yates feared he might faint.

"I'll…I'll just shut the computer down, then I'll be right there."

The man backed out of the office, still clutching the rucksack like it was a barrier between them. Yates glared down at his traitorous cock that was struggling to deflate. The shaking and the waterlogged eyes were usually a turn-on, *want* so palpable it took a man into desperate despair, but not like this.

The guy was scared of him without him trying to scare, and Yates thought about what he must've looked like.

Tucked away in a dark, dank office, groping himself in front of a computer with a flower arrangement screensaver. Yep, he must have looked crazy, and that was before starting on his physical looks. Heat surged into Yates's cheeks. He touched them, gaping at the cause. Embarrassment. Why was he embarrassed? What did it matter this guy thought him odd? Some snotty brat terrified of cock.

He strode out of the office and fixed his eyes on the guy waiting behind the counter. In Yates's peripheral vision, he read Donnie's message and wondered whether the guy had seen it. Was that the reason for his intense reaction? Did he think Yates might attack him with his cock out?

"I locked the door."

The guy's complexion hadn't warmed. His eyes still looked close to falling from his face. Light-brown freckles covered his cheeks and nose. Not small ones, but big freckles, huge even. His eyes were a darker brown, and his hair was too. Yates wondered whether his freckles darkened when he was turned on or if he could blush so bad the red eclipsed them.

The guy's words finally caught up with him, and Yates frowned, folding his arms.

"Why would you lock the door?"

"I'm not here for flowers."

"Okay."

"I'm here for your other expertise."

Yates's cock jolted. *Not you, for fuck's sake.* His blue balls had a mind of their own. The guy's words caught up with Yates again. He tightened his arms, and his frown became harsher. The guy backed up a step before surging forward and knocking into the counter.

"Please."

Fuck. His eyes were watering again, and he said please with a break in his voice. So bloody alluring. The session with Darius was long overdue. Yates rubbed his cock against the side of the counter. Not humping, but itching…

He nodded. "What exactly are we talking about here?"

The guy's brows twitched. Another of Yates's kinks. The facial muscles all firing when the need got too much. It wouldn't have worked if the nose had twitched, or the lips, but the eyebrows... They looked fucking adorable, flexing and tugging while someone begged for release. Yates felt seconds away from tearing the counter apart and launching himself at the guy.

DON'T ATTACK THE CUSTOMERS

"You...kill people, right?"

Yates didn't respond.

"That's what I heard."

"From who?"

He licked his lips. "There's rumors."

"You shouldn't believe all the rumors you hear."

"So, it's not true?"

Yates snorted. "That particular rumor happens to be true."

The guy released a slow breath. "Good, that's good."

Is it?

"I need you to..."

Blow me.

"Yes?"

The guy checked over his shoulder. "I need you to..."

Fuck me.

"Yes?"

"I need you to kill me."

Oh.

The guy started to cry, full-on tears down his freckled cheeks and snot yo-yoing out of his nose, and that was the end of Yates's hard-on. He pulled a tissue from his pocket—that absolutely wasn't there for him to jerk off into—and handed it to the guy bawling on the other side of the counter. Sex, pleasure, desire, lust, Yates could handle those, but emotions, actual emotions... He stared at the guy as he pulled himself together and didn't think much, other than two words...so pathetic.

"What's your name?"

He sniffled. "Why do you want to know?"

"I like to know the names of the people I'm gonna kill."

"Right... It's Dylan."

"Okay, Dylan, how much have you got for me?"

He dumped his rucksack on the counter and rooted around inside. Yates looked. He couldn't help himself. Notebooks, textbooks. One titled *Drama and Theatre*. That made sense. He had an air of the dramatic about him. Dylan retrieved an envelope from the depths of his bag and handed it to Yates.

"It's the rest of my student loan."

Yates peeked inside. A few hundred pounds. A measly amount for an assassin, but it probably seemed a lot for a student.

"How old are you?"

Dylan wiped his face. "Twenty-one."

"And are you sure you want me to do this?"

The tissue dropped from Dylan's hand. He blinked. "You're not gonna ask me why?"

"No."

Dylan swallowed. His eyes darted around the room, stealing glances at the flowers. "You're not gonna talk me out of it?"

"No. I just want to know if you're sure, that's all."

"Right." Dylan licked his lips. Yates found himself staring at them, all shiny and wet. A subtle pink. He wondered what they'd look like after a mauling of a kiss. His cock was hard again. Damn his blue balls. The whole encounter had been humiliating for both of them; Yates just needed it to end.

Dylan lowered his gaze and nipped his bottom lip. Like Yates expected, he began retreating. One step. Two steps. It was a cry for help in the wrong place in front of the wrong person.

Dylan rushed into the counter again.

"I'm sure."

Yates squinted. "Yeah?"

Dylan nodded. "I want it to be quick."

"Okay. Put your hand on the counter."

"What?"

Yates leaned over and spoke close to his ear. "I'm going to use an ancient technique, a pressure point in your hand. It'll stop your heart."

Dylan turned back to the door. Yates waited for him to bolt, but he didn't. He released a slow, shuddering breath.

"But there are people outside."

Cars were whizzing up and down the road, and a man was leaning against the bakery opposite, munching a sausage roll.

"And?"

"I...I don't want you to get into trouble."

Yates tilted his head and studied Dylan. He was breathing fast, still far too pale. Their eyes met, and he didn't look away. His gaze was sincere. He didn't want Yates to get into trouble. The situation was beyond bizarre.

"It'll look like you've had a heart attack, that's all."

"Okay…is it all right if I close my eyes?"

"If you feel more comfortable, I advise it."

It was rare someone stunned Yates, but when Dylan placed his hand on the counter and closed his eyes, he gaped. Why the hell was Dylan so sure he wanted to die? What had he done? Or who was after him? The questions assaulted Yates's mind, but he didn't dare voice them. They felt too much like caring, and he didn't care. Not for emotions, and certainly not for someone so tragic. He'd only just met him, for Christ's sake.

Yates took hold of Dylan's pinkie finger.

Crunch.

Dylan pulled away, screaming. He clutched his hand, gasping for breath. His eyes widened comically as he took in his finger at a completely unnatural angle.

"You broke my finger?"

Yates shoved the envelope in the rucksack. "It's dislocated. The hospital's two miles away. Someone will take pity on you and drive you there. I suggest after they set your finger, you ask to speak to someone."

"Speak to someone?"

Yates held out the rucksack. Dylan took it and slipped it over his shoulder.

"A therapist, a counsellor. Talk to someone, anyone. Just make sure they care."

Because he sure as hell didn't.

CHAPTER TWO

Yates gazed at the bunch of yellow flowers bouncing as he walked, completely at odds with the grey skies and drizzle dropping down around them. Flowers made the summer. The sun liked to play peekaboo and piss everyone off, but the flowers were bright no matter what. Forever vibrant and cheerful. Even at funerals. No one brought dark flowers to a funeral.

The receptionist stopped Yates in his tracks.

"You can't bring those in the hospital."

She eyed the flowers like he'd walked into the hospital with a bouquet of lice-infested rats. When he turned to show her, she recoiled, knocking a stack of files off her desk.

"They're for a friend."

"They pose a health risk."

If anything, surely flowers brightened people's spirits? Yates found them uplifting, and he was a self-proclaimed misery.

Yates looked down at them. "What do you think patients might do? Swallow them? Cut themselves on their leaves? Inhale the pollen? Strangle themselves on the stems?"

The receptionist lifted her chin, all defiant and self-righteous. But Yates didn't miss the way she flashed a look at the security guard on the door. "Well, actually, it's to do with the bacteria in the water when plants are left—"

"Save it," Yates growled, dropping them on the counter.

"You can't leave them there."

"Then what am I supposed to do with them?"

She pointed at the doors. "Leave them outside."

"This is a twenty-five quid bouquet."

"Get a cheaper bunch next time."

He told himself to breathe slowly through his mouth, not fast through his nose.

Yates stalked outside and threw them down on a bench. He sighed and rearranged them to snap a picture on his phone. When he went back inside, glaring at the receptionist, she held her palm up at him again.

"What now?"

"Sorry." She smiled. "The shirt, I thought you were still carrying flowers."

Someone's a fucking comedian.

Yates said nothing and breezed by the desk without waiting for her to welcome him in. The labyrinth of corridors boggled his mind, and when he finally located Edna, he imagined he'd aged a few years. Edna looked like she had, not years but decades.

"I love the shirt."

Yates ran his hands down his chest, not cotton but satin. He'd been pleased with his purchase, but not everybody was a fan, and boy, did they like to tell him.

"I brought you some flowers, your favorites."

The ones she stared at the most but never bought.

"Sadly, they don't allow them inside."

He forced a smile on his face, a sprinkle of mock cheer in his voice, but on the inside, he mentally tore the hospital to pieces. Edna struggled up in bed and waved him closer. Her fingers were so skinny a handshake would've snapped them.

"Were they yellow?"

"Of course."

Her face hung with sadness. Yates didn't miss her glance at the bedside cabinet, nothing colorful on top. The décor in the hospital was downright depressing.

"That's a shame," Edna said. "Yellow's such a cheerful color."

Yates pointed at his sunflowers. "Tell me about it. I took a picture, though; I know it's not the same."

She reached for her glasses on the table. They hung on a string, and Yates helped her get it over her head. When she glanced at Yates, he jerked back at her bloodshot eyes, magnified by the inch-thick glasses.

"What?"

"You look like some crazy professor."

She slapped his arm and stuck out her chin towards the phone. "Come on then. Let's see them."

Yates showed her the photo of the flowers on the bench. Edna awwed as if she was looking at kittens or a baby. Her frail hand pressed over her equally frail heart, much like the pose Ranger had done earlier in the shop.

"They're beautiful."

Yates had made sure of it. The best bunch in the shop. Love, Yates didn't get, but beauty... He understood that. He'd made sure to pick stunners.

"Better than supermarket bought?"

"No question about it."

Edna took the phone in her shaking grip and studied the flowers. She scrolled to the next picture and grimaced just as Yates snatched the phone from her.

"What was that?"

A sex toy unboxing video.

"Nothing for you to worry about, some silicone kitchen spoon."

"Interesting color."

Yates nodded. He agreed with Edna. It was probably the first bright-green vibrator he'd seen. "It glows in the dark."

Edna rubbed her head. "Why would you be cooking in the dark?"

Oh.

"How are you feeling, Edna?"

"Sore, that's all." She grinned at Yates. "I can't complain, really. I've had a good life overall."

What was he supposed to say to that?

"It's still going on, Edna."

"I know, but you know as well as I do this fall might be it. If I were to die, I just want it known I had a good life."

Yates sat down beside her. "So, I met your granddaughter's boyfriend."

Edna's face soured. "Right scrounging bastard, isn't he?"

Yates smiled, not forced, but genuine. If he had a favorite customer, Edna would be it, but alas, favoring someone over another involved emotion, and he lacked those.

Edna made him snort more than anyone else, though. That meant he must like her, the same way he liked Ranger and Donnie.

He sat beside her and listened to her bitch about Adam, and then she recalled the tale of how she hurt her hip, then her husband's love of vintage cars. Even if he'd wanted to speak, she didn't allow him any room. It was a continuous stream of a one-sided conversation until her eyes shut, and Yates thought she'd drifted off.

He grabbed his jacket off the back of the chair and got to his feet.

"You're a good-looking man, you know that?"

"And your eyesight is getting poorer every day."

"True." She opened her eyes and winked. "But it's still not that bad that I'd mistake a dildo for a silicone spoon."

Yates's smile grew to painful proportions. "Vibrator, actually."

"What's the difference?"

"This specific one is to hit your prostate. It's called the annihilator."

Edna pointed to the exit. "Get the hell out of here, dirty dog."

****

The flowers had vanished from the bench, and as Yates looked up and down the road, he spotted them in the hands of a man standing at a bus stop. He wasn't facing Yates, but the yellow bursts of color were obvious over his shoulder. Yates didn't march over and grab them. He let them go.

The guy was probably heading back to his romantic partner, and Yates imagined it would be a nice surprise until they read the label. 'To my bit on the side.'

It would've made Edna laugh; Yates was sure of it, but the man's partner… Yates prayed for fireworks. What he'd give to be a tarantula on the wall. Tarantula, not fly; he'd never lower himself to a fly. He chuckled at his thoughts.

"Oh my God, have you seen him?"

Yates gritted his teeth. No doubt he was the 'him' the shrill voice referred to. The red patches on his face weren't exactly flattering, but they didn't deserve to be called out in the street.

"I was in a fire," he snapped, turning to her.

The woman had her hand slapped over her mouth. She glanced at Yates, then resumed staring at the roof of the hospital. Yates followed her gaze and froze at the sight of Dylan on the roof.

The blood leached from his face. "Oh, fuck."

Yates took off in a sprint through the whirling maze of a hospital until he found the stairwell. He took the steps two at a time and busted through the door onto the roof.

"What the hell are you doing?"

The boom of his voice made Dylan jump, teasing the drop below. He swayed. Yates looked down at Dylan's undone shoelaces. Whether he tripped or jumped, it looked like he'd go over the edge.

"Fucking Jesus," Yates gasped, running his hands through his hair. He felt different; he felt twitchy and on edge, and when he took his pulse at his wrist, it was racing.

What the hell was happening to him?

Dylan shot a look over his shoulder. "You're the flower shop man?"

"Huh? Yes. My name is Yates; now back away from the edge."

His heart thundered in his chest, beating so hard he swore it put a shake in his voice.

"Are you going to ask why I'm up here?"

"I'm not qualified to ask, but someone downstairs will be."

Yates inched closer, his arms out and ready in case he needed to leap. He flexed his fingers, testing his clutch. Was he strong enough? Fast enough? Jesus, he'd never doubted himself before.

"Why don't you just try it?"

"Try what?" Yates asked.

Dylan looked out at the horizon. "Asking me why."

"I'm not good at this sort of stuff." Yates stopped, but hell, he could try. He could pretend he cared to save someone's life. "Why are you up here, Dylan?"

Dylan glanced over his shoulder. "Well, actually, I'm glad you asked."

He chuckled, *chuckled*, then he stared straight down at the street beneath. "He ended it with me. I mean, he'd already ended it, but he ended it again when I asked to see him."

Yates's eyes fluttered. He squeezed them shut, letting the words sink in. This was a cry for help over an ended relationship. Heartbreak, most people went through it at some point. Unrequited love or unrequited friendship. It happened. Yates hadn't experienced it himself, not that he'd never been dumped. It just didn't affect him. Ending it all because of that, at the tender age of twenty-one. It seemed a pathetic reason.

So pathetic.

Yates shut that voice down. That was why he was rubbish with this kind of stuff. He was emotionally dead, but others weren't. They cared, they cried, they hurt.

"I love him."

"This is beyond my capability."

"Are you a robot?"

He sighed. "Sometimes I wonder."

Dylan turned around. "You must've loved someone?"

"Come away from the edge."

"Answer me."

"I love sex, I love money, I love flowers. They're things, not people. Life is easier that way."

"That's kind of...cold."

Yates shrugged. "We are who we are."

"It wasn't a healthy relationship."

"Maybe he's done you a favor."

Dylan licked his lips. "I think I'm upset he ended it but more upset that I wasn't the one to end it first. Does that make sense?"

No.

"It might make sense, perfect sense, but more so if you came away from the edge."

"Like, it makes me a worse person because I wasn't the one to walk away. He took that away from me too, so I'm the bad one."

"Look, kid, I don't know what it is you want me to say."

"I don't want you to say anything. I just want someone to listen."

He'd endured hours from Edna. A few minutes listening to Dylan wasn't too much to ask, right?

"Go ahead."

"If he calls me or turns up at my flat, I'll be all over him. I have no willpower. I'm already hoping he'll change his mind again, ask to see me. That makes me a bad person, the worst."

His voice broke, and Yates felt it in his chest. It weakened him. That or he was experiencing a cardiac arrest. The idea of the latter appealed to him more.

"On God's earth, I don't think you could ever be a bad person."

"I think I'd surprise you. I feel bad for not breaking up with him first, bad for wanting him to change his mind, and bad for crying if he doesn't. I don't know what I'm supposed to do now. I don't know how to pretend to be happy while feeling like I'm being torn apart inside."

"Fuck pretending, if you're feeling miserable, feel miserable, but for God's sake, talk to someone."

"You said you'd just listen."

"Sorry," Yates said, lifting his hands in surrender.

"I don't want to bring anyone else down. I don't want to make them unhappy, but it's hard when you feel like shit and there's happiness all around you. When you've got to smile and be this certain person everyone expects you to be. It's exhausting."

Yates held out his hand. "There's people downstairs who you can talk to."

"You're talking to me."

"They're trained for this. Anything I say will be more likely to make you jump than change your mind."

"Jump?" Dylan looked down at the road below. "You think I'm gonna jump?"

"It looks like that, yeah."

Dylan stepped away from the edge, and Yates let loose a huge sigh.

"I wasn't going to jump."

"Right…"

"No, really I wasn't."

"What were you doing?"

"I was watching."

"The road?"

"Yeah."

Yates crossed his arms. "But you did come to my shop and ask me to kill you?"

Dylan said nothing.

"Come on." Yates waved him closer. "Let's get you talking with someone."

Dylan picked up his rucksack from the roof and slung it over his shoulder. "Someone who cares."

"Exactly. That person isn't me."

As soon as he was within reach, Yates hooked his arm over Dylan's shoulders and marched him to the door. He sighed right down Dylan's neck. It left him woozy.

"Why did you come up here then?"

Yates pushed Dylan inside, and out of his view, he frowned. *Why had he run up there?* Why was his heart jackhammering in his chest? He pressed his hand against it, slowing now Dylan was away from the edge. *Strange.*

"I didn't want you to make a mess on the pavement."

Dylan sneaked a sidewards look at him. "Did you come to the hospital to check on me?"

There was such hope in Dylan's voice Yates thought about lying, but he didn't.

"Nope, I'd forgotten all about you until I saw you on the roof."

He'd been on Yates's mind in the immediate aftermath of their encounter at the shop, all until Yates jerked off in the office thinking of him, then he was gone. Teary eyes, twitching eyebrows, huge freckles—all gone.

Now here they were, Yates ushering Dylan through the hospital in case he might dive out of the closest window, his heavy hand on Dylan's shoulder, not to comfort him, but to grab him at a moment's notice.

"Why are you here then?"

"I was visiting a friend."

"You have friends?"

Yates snorted. "Hard to believe I know."

"What happened to them?"

"She slipped on a banana skin and busted her hip."

"Good one." Dylan laughed.

Yates stopped Dylan and growled in his ear. "I'm not joking."

He genuinely wasn't. That was how Edna had hurt her hip. They'd both laughed their heads off when she'd told him, but Dylan wasn't in on the joke. He didn't get to laugh at Edna's comedic failure.

"Let's get you sorted out." He ruffled Dylan's hair before strangling his wrist and glaring at his hand. It had a mind of its own. Stroking Dylan's hair. He may have leaned into the touch, but it was a weird reaction for both of them.

Getting someone to speak with Dylan wasn't as easy as Yates had envisioned. He was put on a waiting list and given a list of numbers to call if he was feeling suicidal. Not good enough in Yates's eyes, but huffing and puffing out his chest seemed to have absolutely no effect on the doctor sat opposite.

Dr Nick narrowed his eyes. "Do you need something?"

"Like what?"

"Some water."

"I don't want water. I want Dylan to speak to someone."

"As I said, we're in the middle of a mental health crisis."

"Can't you get him admitted somewhere?"

Dylan sprang off his chair like he'd been electrocuted. "Admitted?"

"Yeah, locked away so you can't hurt yourself."

Even Dr Nick looked disgusted. Yates rolled his eyes. He'd said something unacceptable again and not even realized it. Pretending to care was hard.

"I don't understand why what I said is bad?"

"I'm not an animal. You can't lock me away."

"I'm thinking of ways of keeping you alive."

He kicked Yates's foot. "I'm not suicidal anymore."

"That's what a suicidal person would say."

Dr Nick slumped back in his chair and squeezed the bridge of his nose.

"Maybe you'd like to wait outside and allow me to speak to Dylan alone?"

Yates nodded. He got up and turned to Dylan. "Good luck, kid."

"What? You're not leaving, are you?"

Yates checked his watch. Darius was due over at his place in a few hours. He needed to eat, shower, and change the bed sheets. Sex was always better on a blank canvas. "Yeah—"

"He said to wait outside."

Yates stared at where Dylan had grabbed hold of him. The hem of his sunflower print shirt. His eyebrows twitched, his eyes darted, and Yates inwardly cursed. That wasn't fair. Dylan was playing *dirty* and didn't even know it.

"Will you wait?"

"For a couple of minutes."

Dylan swallowed; Yates heard it. The slow bob of his throat. He clutched the bottom of Yates shirt with both hands, begging with his eyes and his adorable eyebrows.

"Please, Yates."

Motherfucker.

"Fine, I'll wait. Then afterward, I'll give you a ride home, but that's it, okay?"

Relief and gratitude brought color to Dylan's face. He smiled, the first smile Yates had seen, and it was directed at him. He stared, not knowing how to react, before ruffling Dylan's hair. It tickled through his fingers like strands of silk. He'd lost his mind, but Dylan didn't back away from the lunatic stroking him like a dog; he beamed.

"Thank you."

CHAPTER THREE

Dylan didn't speak on the drive to his student halls, much to Yates's relief. He'd had enough human interaction to last him a week, and the hospital experience had confirmed what he already knew. He preferred the company of flowers. They didn't ask stupid questions or have annoying laughs. They didn't point at him or openly gossip about how he'd gotten his scars. Most of the time, Yates dealt with assholes by getting in their face and intimidating them, but he'd refrained from punching anyone at the hospital. Just that once. Dylan needed a ride home after all.

Dylan curled into the side of the car door, resting his head on his rucksack. His eyes were closed, and his breathing came evenly. It calmed Yates to see him like that, which made absolutely no sense. He'd known Dylan for barely a few hours, but there was something about his vulnerability that tugged on Yates's one remaining heartstring.

He clawed at his chest, wanting to reach inside and snap it.

Dylan's phone buzzed, and he was startled awake. Yates's heart punched faster at the sudden break in calm. He strangled the wheel and huffed. Dare he say it, he'd been enjoying the ride. Dylan yawned and checked the message. If they hadn't been stopped at traffic lights, Yates wouldn't have looked over, but he did and stored the text in his head to dissect later.

Friday, Greenhill, 20:00. We can still be friends x

Dylan slid his hand down his face and dropped his phone back in his rucksack.

"That him?"

He nodded. "That's him."

"Want me to call him and tell him to fuck off?"

"You'd absolutely terrify him."

Yates lowered his eyes to slits and glowered at Dylan. *Here it comes.* The kid had gone almost the whole day without mentioning his appearance. "And why's that, huh?"

"You're so…"

Scarred.

"So?"

Dylan licked his lips. "You're so…"

Inked.

"Yes?"

"You're so big."

Yates turned his attention back to the road. *Big?* Tall, wide, and muscly, he *was* big, but most people noticed the red patches on his face and the tattoos disappearing under the neck of his shirt. They didn't appreciate the hard work he put in at the gym to have his physique. But truthfully, they probably didn't notice once they locked eyes on his shirts. They definitely had the wow factor.

"I'm bigger than your ex?"

Dylan screwed up his face. "Don't call him that…and yes, easily."

The thrill of being declared alpha male only lasted for a few seconds. Dylan, the twenty-one-year-old drama student had called him big. His not-ex was probably a student too, scrawny and half-starved. Not much of a compliment, after all. Yates sighed and jabbed his finger at the building in front.

"This yours, Annabelle House?"

Dylan nodded. "That's the one."

He pulled over and twisted in his seat to face Dylan. "You've got friends inside, right?"

"Yes."

"And family out there somewhere?"

Dylan nodded. "I've got a sister."

"Talk to them. I'm sure you know someone who's been through the same thing. They can give you some advice. Help you deal with whatever it is you're going through."

He forced a smile, expecting Dylan to slip out of the car after his words of wisdom, but he didn't. Dylan hugged his rucksack, not looking at Yates but over his shoulder at nothing.

"Hey…" Yates leaned over and ruffled his hair. "Go on."

By some miracle, they were the magic words. Dylan woke up from wherever he'd momentarily gone and smiled.

"Thank you," he said, finally opening the door. Dylan climbed out and ducked his head down. "I love the shirt."

Yates inflated his chest, congratulating his shirt on a job well done. Two genuine compliments in one day. That was a record.

"Daffodils are my favorite."

Dylan slammed the door and ran off in the direction of Annabelle House. Distracted by his arse, it took a while for Yates's brain to process Dylan's parting words.

"Idiot." His nostrils flared. "They're not daffodils. They're sunflowers."

He watched until Dylan disappeared inside, then watched a little longer to make sure he didn't appear on the roof. Yates's fingers were tacky from where he'd touched Dylan's hair, and he idly rubbed them together. He smelled like strawberries, like he'd been in a rush and not washed all his shampoo out. So sweet Yates's mouth watered.

Yates froze when he realized his eyes were shut and his hand was over his mouth and nose. He pulled it away, ashamed he'd been sniffing and drooling over it like an addict. He needed to cure his blue balls. He needed to get laid.

He needed Darius.

Yates's phone buzzed in his pocket, and for a second, he thought Darius had read his mind, but instead it was an alert about the next best thing, Mr Stevenson.

****

"You know I had to cancel a date for this, right?"

Yates threw a glance back at Ranger. "No, you didn't."

"How the hell would you know?"

"You text me whenever you've got a date."

Ranger huffed. "Fine, I didn't have a date, but being here with you means I can't have a date tonight, and what if he was the one, huh? You could've cost me my happiness."

Yates ignored him and gestured to his phone. The camera he'd rigged to one of Mr Stevenson's many properties had finally picked up his car before going blank. Any normal hit, Yates would've observed from afar, got an idea of Mr Stevenson's habits, and struck at the opportune moment. That's how his tactical brain worked. His skills as a military strategist had always given him good results, not with only his hits but Donnie's and Ranger's. The flower shop assassins always got their marks…eventually. *Minus Elliot.*

Mr Stevenson wasn't a normal hit, though. He had a knack for disappearing, overly aware there were people out in the world who wanted him dead.

"The car's still there," Yates mumbled. He turned when Ranger didn't answer and found him pulling up clover and spearing it through his hair.

"It's hard to imagine you're a killer."

Ranger pointed at his head. "Really? I'm killing it now."

"As I was saying"—Yates snapped his fingers to gain Ranger's attention, then pointed to the house—"his car is still there, and the lights are on."

"Maybe your camera just…died."

"It's military grade."

Ranger rolled his eyes. "Military stuff still breaks, take you, for example."

"I'm not broken," Yates growled. "I left on my own accord."

"Whatever."

Yates reached over and brushed his fingers aggressively through his hair. Ranger's hair wasn't soft, or silky like Dylan's, and it didn't smell of strawberries but distinctly of Ranger. Not a bad smell, but not Dylan's smell. *Goddamn it.* Yates needed to concentrate and not think about strawberry-scented hair and watery eyes.

Ranger yelped and caught the clover in his hands. "That was mean."

"I need you focused."

"Fine. Can we get it over with?"

Military Yates would've demanded they wait longer, observe from a distance, but this hit was time sensitive with Mr Stevenson vanishing all the time. He needed it done. Yates nodded and rushed forward. He kicked the front door open. It swung, battering the wall and breaking off the plaster. Ranger had a gun in each hand and at least ten knives strapped around his body. His nostrils pulsed, and he pushed Yates aside as he went into the house.

"I smell food."

"Goddamn it, Ranger, that is not how you storm a building."

"We're not storming a building; we're killing one guy. Let's hurry up and find him, then investigate the food situation. I'm starving."

He bounded off into the house, not a care for a trap or the possibility of an armed Mr Stevenson.

"Erm…Yates?"

Yates rushed toward the sound of his voice and ended up, unsurprisingly, in the kitchen. Ranger pointed at the table and the note written on top.

Almost had him…

"Fuck," Yates snapped, tearing out of the room. He searched the house from top to bottom before returning to the kitchen. He glared until his eyes nearly popped out. Ranger had found the source of the smell and pulled a roast chicken from the oven.

"Ta-dah! Carrots, potatoes, parsnips, gravy. We hit the jackpot."

"The jackpot would've been Mr Stevenson."

"Point taken, but this is a close second."

Yates tried to calm his temper as Ranger set up the table. He dished up two plates of food while whistling a happy tune.

"Join me."

"Are you for real?"

"Hey, it will go to waste otherwise."

Yates lurched forward and flung his plate across the room. Vegetables, chicken, and gravy splattered on the floor. Ranger's easy-going smile faded as he wrapped a possessive arm around his plate. "You do that to mine; I'll kill you."

Not a threat to be taken lightly. His eyes found Yates, and he saw him barely hanging on to the anger. They were evenly matched in size and muscle, but Ranger was an animal when he lost control. Unfeeling of pain or fatigue, frothing at the mouth, and with no memory of the events afterward. Yates took a few slow breaths before sitting down opposite Ranger.

Ranger flashed him a crooked smile, then loaded a gravy-covered carrot into his mouth.

"They could've poisoned that."

"Doesn't taste like poison."

Yates closed his eyes, counting to ten. "The point is you wouldn't know it was poison until it was too late."

"Huh…" Ranger bit into a potato. "Well, I've started now, might as well finish." He waved his half-finished potato to the note. "Your thoughts?"

"Mr Stevenson has hired help." Yates glanced around. "They must've left quickly, too quickly."

"That's obvious; dinner's still cooking. Who leaves before dinner?"

"That's not what I meant. If it was me, and I had more time, I would've booby-trapped the house. The camera's only been disabled for twenty minutes. They must've taken it out, then driven Mr Stevenson to another location."

"Where?"

"If I knew that, we'd be there too!"

"Okay, okay, don't get your panties in a twist."

"I swear, Ranger…"

Ranger snorted. "What do you swear?"

"I will ram a fork through your cock before you get a chance to kill me." Yates pulled out his phone and scrolled through his contacts.

"Do you speak to your old army bitches like that?"

"Quiet."

He pressed down on a name and only had to wait for two rings before it answered.

"What do you need help with?"

"My man got away. He's hired outside help, and rather stupidly, one of them wrote me a taunting note."

"Snap me a picture and send it over."

"Thanks, Seth."

"Anytime, Yates, anytime."

He took a picture of the note, then turned his attention to Ranger. "I speak to them politely because they show me respect."

"And they respect you because you saved their lives."

"Multiple times and I still would if they ever needed me to."

Ranger pushed out his bottom lip. "You're making me jealous."

"Of what?"

"All the orgies you must've had in the army. Hot and sticky while you rolled around in the sand. It's getting me hard underneath the table."

"You're sick."

Ranger laughed. "I'm sexually frustrated, even while eating chicken."

"Hurry up and finish so we can leave." Yates smacked his lips together. "So that's what it tastes like."

"What?"

"Failure. It's bitter and disappointing. No wonder Donnie turned to alcohol. It seems to be the place to turn to when life goes wrong and you want to make it even more unbearable."

Ranger waved his knife toward Yates. "You need to give Donnie more credit. He gave it up; not everyone can."

Yates said nothing.

****

Lights flashed around them. The music pumped from the speakers and vibrated the floor. Yates hadn't ventured inside a club like this for years, all bright colors and laser lights. It was garish, and loud, and didn't stock whiskey. It was *hell*.

He downed a shot of something sticky and turned to Ranger.

"What do you think the alcohol volume is on these?"

Ranger cracked a smile. "Sweet fuck-all. They taste like watered-down squash."

Yates agreed, but he preferred the shots to the fluorescent alcohol pops. He would not be seen clutching one of those plastic bottles. Without a doubt, Ranger would snap a picture and send it to Donnie.

"Why are we here?" Ranger asked.

"I needed a distraction from Mr Stevenson, and you complained you were sexually frustrated a few days ago. I'm helping you in your quest to get laid."

"Excuse me, I can get laid. That's not the problem. I want them to stay in the morning without needing to chain them to the bed."

"No chains, no fun." He thought of Darius, tied up and begging. He'd cured Yates's blue balls and put a mental block on Dylan, but over the course of the week, the block had faded. It had come away to reveal Dylan's tragic face, twisty eyebrows and all.

"Why here?"

Greenhill. A cheap nightclub. One dance floor. One karaoke room. Two bars. A toilet that leaked the smell of urine into the club after midnight. That's what a review said, at least.

Yates hated it when he found the place online and hated it even more when he strolled through the doors.

"You weren't having much luck finding a guy. I thought you'd have more luck here. Somewhere a bit different."

Ranger swiveled his stool to face the dance floor. "See, I'd get that if there was anyone here."

Yates scrunched his face up. Ranger had a point.

The club was empty, other than the bar staff who tried to keep their distance. Every time Yates gestured one over, he threw a look back to his friends as if he might not return.

"Why did we come here at 19:30?"

Yates had wanted to arrive before Dylan, get a good vigil position, and observe from afar. He wasn't there to interact or be seen. He wanted to know Dylan was all right, that was all. Knowing that would cure him of the odd prickly sensation in his gut.

Yates didn't answer Ranger, and Ranger knew not to push him.

"What do you think?" Ranger sprung up from his stool and ran his hands down his shirt. A plain white shirt. Plain grey jeans. Plain black shoes. He waited for Yates's approval with a pleased smile, but Yates didn't return it. He despised ordinary.

Yates looked away. "I prefer your low-hanging vest tops that flash your pecs and your head shaved to show that mean tattoo of yours."

Yates hated to admit it, but he was jealous of Ranger's tattoo. All the ink he'd had done, and he saw the perfect tattoo on his mate's head.

"I want to look...normal."

"Why?"

Ranger grabbed a handful of his hair that covered his tattoo. "Because this doesn't attract the right kinda guy."

"What's your plan? Seduce someone *normal*, and slowly over a few months reveal you're batshit crazy and kill people for a living?"

Ranger put his hands on his hips. "You got a better idea?"

"I would say be yourself, but fucking hell. We're friends, and I barely tolerate you."

"Right back at you."

Ranger picked his next shot glass of the bar and held it up to Yates. They clinked their glasses together before downing the contents. More sickly-sweet water. They both grimaced.

Ranger looked at him. "We're gonna need to drink gallons of this before we feel something."

"The goal is not to get smashed."

"I know, but this place is a dive. Why don't we go to The Archer?"

"No," Yates growled. "I want to stay here."

Ranger stared at him. A hint of anger flashed in his eyes, and Yates braced himself. It faded, and Ranger sat back down on the stool. It wouldn't have been ideal if Dylan strolled inside while Ranger was having one of his moments and they were brawling on the floor.

"Okay, but if there's no one here in thirty minutes, we're leaving."

"Deal."

Another thing Yates hated to admit to. If Ranger was having one of his red moments, he'd beat Yates into next week.

Luckily for Ranger, the club got busier and as they sat at the bar, they had the perfect spot to watch the steady stream of clubbers coming inside. Yates watched too, more subtly than Ranger, who grinned like a Cheshire cat.

Dylan didn't show up.

Yates stayed by the bar and checked the time on his phone throughout the night, but Dylan didn't make an appearance. He reasoned it was a good thing.

He didn't follow people he wasn't going to kill; he wasn't a weirdo.

Yates downed what was probably his thirtieth shot and tried to find Ranger. The different club and normal clothes had attracted a lot of interest for Ranger throughout the night. Yates suspected it was because Ranger was older, more mature, and the horny students stared after him with their tongues lolling out. They flocked to him, desperate to introduce themselves and get Ranger's number, and he got high off the attention.

Yates had the opposite effect. The students backed away or whispered behind their hands while they looked at him. They feared him more than Ranger, which was ridiculous. Ranger had killed a lot more people and a lot more recently than Yates, but *killer* didn't come to mind when looking at Ranger.

He was too smiley and bouncy.

A cocker spaniel.

"Enjoying yourself?" Yates asked.

His scary face dispersed Ranger's group of admirers. He didn't seem bothered though, in fact, he flashed Yates a blissful smile.

"This place is great. I think the stag party is finally off the karaoke machine. Want to duet with me?"

Yates scrunched up his face. "Not a chance in hell."

"Damn, I'll have to find someone else."

"You've got a whole choir worth of guys desperate to sing with you."

Ranger lifted his eyebrow. "Great, isn't it?"

Yates glanced over to the exit. "I'm gonna get a taxi home."

"You sure?"

"I'm sure." He punched Ranger on the shoulder. "I'll see you later."

"I'll swing by the shop tomorrow."

Yates rolled his eyes as he strolled away.

No doubt it would be the beaten dog version of Ranger who graced the shop the next morning.

Yates showing up at Greenhill had been weird at best and downright stalkerish at worst.

Dylan not turning up was a good thing for Yates and a good thing for Dylan. It meant he hadn't accepted the olive branch to be friends with his ex; he'd ignored him.

Not so pathetic after all.

CHAPTER FOUR

The lungful of fresh air outside the club was as close to heaven as Yates was ever going to get. His ears fizzled, and the sweet shots he'd been drinking endlessly sloshed in his stomach.

He hadn't missed those kinds of clubs, and he vowed never to visit one again. Tomorrow, it was back to business. Flower business and other business. He hoped to open his emails on some useful intel about Mr Stevenson. Seth was gifted, more than capable of finding a man from his handwriting over the internet. Electronic signatures were everywhere, and he'd messaged to say the owner of the handwriting had unique a and s formations.

Yates jogged across the road to call a cab. A group of rowdy students went past, and he was forced to back into an alley just to be able to hear the guy on the phone. Ten minutes.

He sighed, pocketing his phone, and threw a look down the alley. Rustling and suction noises came from behind a huge wheely bin. Yates grimaced. Sex clubs got a seedy reputation they didn't deserve. From Yates's experience, they were tasteful and respectful.

Cheap night clubs, on the other hand, were dirty. He shuddered, turning his back on the alley to await his taxi. The wheely bin crashed into the wall. Someone cursed. Yates stiffened at fabric tearing. That was the other thing about sex clubs; consensual sex was a big must.

Yates crept down the alley, wanting to gauge the mood of whoever was getting it on at the end. Tearing clothes didn't always mean something sinister. Yates loved ripping shirts with his sexual partners.

He inched closer and went rigid. He didn't move, but something uncomfortable inflated inside his chest, something huge that seemed to fill him up.

Dylan, leaning against the wall, having his neck thoroughly slobbered over. His eyes were shut, his lips slightly parted, and he didn't look like he wasn't enjoying himself. He moaned, big and beautiful; Yates felt it too. Vibrating through the air.

He swallowed and stared.

The guy groped, and touched, and muttered into Dylan's throat. His lips smacked, somehow louder than the fuzz in Yates's ears. He hated the noise, but he didn't intervene. This was young men getting off in an alley. Yates, Ranger, and Donnie had done it tons of times when they were that age. It was natural and kinda hot.

He should absolutely walk away and give them privacy.

Except he couldn't.

Yates couldn't drag his gaze away from Dylan.

Dylan's head lolled to the side, unsteady on his shoulders. His eyebrow twitched; he breathed hard and fast. Fuck, he got Yates's heart pounding, a different kind of pounding to the rooftop. His skin heated up, too hot. He wanted to pick at the buttons of his shirt, get some air on his chest. He wanted to rip his shirt from his body and pounce like a tiger. Whatever the slobbery man was doing, Yates could do it better.

Dylan's knees gave out a little, making him slip down the wall. Yates bit his lip to stop his groan and shoved at his straining cock. The man pulled Dylan back into position on the wall and then resumed rutting up against him.

He really shouldn't be watching this. He had to get out of the alley. It was a miracle Dylan hadn't seen him yet. Yates touched himself, over his jeans, but the sensation was electric.

Dylan drifted sideways again, knocking into the wheely bin. The man dry humping him cursed and hauled Dylan upright again.

Dylan, who was indeed red-cheeked and moaning softly, didn't react other than to pant. His arms hung at his sides; his head tipped forward. His eyes stayed shut.

Yates stopped touching himself and gaped. Dread filled his chest and flowed out of him into a growl.

Dylan was fucking intoxicated.

"Piece of shit," Yates yelled, rushing into action.

He yanked the man off Dylan and threw him down, kicked him twice in the stomach, then caught Dylan before he dropped to the floor. Yates hauled Dylan up and tried to get a good look at him, but his head was tipping and swaying all over the place.

"Hey," he said, gripping Dylan's chin to keep him still. "Open your eyes."

Dylan continued to breathe hard and fast. His lashes fluttered as he tried to open them.

Yates's thigh rested between Dylan's legs, and he could feel that he was absolutely not hard. Yates was, just a little, with the waning bit of arousal that refused to vanish with Dylan looking back at him. Even in the dull light of the alley, Yates could see Dylan's pupils were blown and darting all over the place.

"You, okay?"

It was a stupid question, completely stupid, and Yates hated stupid questions, but there he was, asking it. Dylan's eyes rolled back into his head. Yates shook him lightly, and they came down again, dazed and unseeing.

"Christ," Yates growled, turning to the man on the floor. He'd gone. Yates twisted to face the other way and spotted him crawling away. He'd got to the entrance of the alley. He hadn't got a good look at his face but narrowed his eyes at the cheap-looking tattoo on the back of his neck. Barbed wire. He wished he had some at hand to wrap around the guy's neck for real.

"What did you give him, you arsehole!"

The man got up and ran, and if it wasn't for Dylan so unsteady on his feet and vulnerable, Yates would've given chase. He would have beaten the shit out of him and called Ranger to join him.

Dylan pushed off the wall and rammed his face into Yates's throat. He got comfortable, pressing against Yates's chest and sighing softly into his shoulder.

Yates let him.

"I'm gonna take you to the hospital."

"Don't."

Yates looked down, saw Dylan weakly lifting his arms. They slid around Yates in a feeble hug. Yates pulled him away from the wall and hugged him back.

"Take me home, just this once."

His hair smelled of strawberries. He cursed Dylan for tainting strawberries. He wouldn't be able to eat one anymore without thinking of Dylan, and he wasn't comfortable with the idea.

"I knew…"

Dylan mumbled the rest of his words into Yates's neck. He frowned and leaned Dylan back so he could hear.

"What did you say?"

"I knew you'd ask for me back."

A tear ran over his cheek, then he closed his eyes. He put the last of his remaining strength into his arms to hug Yates harder before passing out.

Ask for me back?

Oh.

"I'm not your… 'not-ex', you hear me?"

Dylan didn't reply. When Yates leaned him back, he had his eyes shut and a huge dopey grin on his face.

"You're so pathetic."

****

Yates stiffened when Dylan flopped into his lap in the back of the cab. He gritted his teeth and mentally prepared for the vomit to flow down his leg. It wasn't Dylan's fault. It was the arsehole's in the alley. The driver threw them irritated glances in the mirror. Yates didn't blame him. The prospect of vomit filling the car didn't appeal to him either.

They waited, but Dylan surprised them both by not spewing everywhere.

Dylan rested his cheek on Yates's thigh and deflated with a slow sigh. Not sick. *Yet.* Yates relaxed into his seat, and the driver stopped flashing him evil looks. It wouldn't take long to get to Yates's place with the empty roads and the driver keeping his foot firmly on the gas. There was a timebomb on the backseat, after all, Dylan's stomach.

Yates watched Dylan on his thigh, each streetlamp they whizzed past lighting his face for a split second. He looked so small on Yates's huge thigh, seemed so helpless puffing out slow breaths in the quiet of the car. Yates hovered his hand above Dylan's head before snatching it back. He needed to put a stop to the hair petting.

"This you?"

Yates dragged his gaze from Dylan and looked out the windscreen. "Yes, this is us."

He paid the driver, then helped Dylan from the car. He swayed, knocking into the cab before overcompensating and ending up in a bush. The more Dylan tried to lift himself out, the more he sank into it like a burrowing animal.

"Christ," Yates hissed.

He picked Dylan up over his shoulder and ambled towards the front door. He shuddered, bracing himself for the vomit to rush down the back of his jeans and into his arse crack, but the vomit stayed put in Dylan's stomach. *For now.*

"I want to sleep."

"Well, it just so happens I've got a nice comfy bed for you," Yates said, shifting him slightly. He hooked his keys from his pocket and unlocked the door. "Try not to vomit on it; I've just changed the sheets."

Dylan grunted. It didn't fill Yates with any confidence.

He carried Dylan through the house, flicking on light switches as he went, and dumped him on the bed. Dylan spread out like a starfish with his eyes shut. Leaves and twigs stuck out of his hair from where he'd tried to hibernate inside Yates's front bush. He leaned over and picked them out before dropping them in the trash can by the bed.

"You okay?"

Dylan grunted again.

He was safe, breathing soundly, so vulnerable in this state it made Yates want to pick him up and shake him. Anyone could've stolen him in the night. Anyone could have hurt him. If Yates hadn't found him down the alley... A growl rumbled in the back of his throat, and he shook the thoughts away. The guy in the alley would be long gone; no point trying to hunt him down.

Yates gritted his teeth when he noticed the red hickey on Dylan's skin. The arsehole in the alley had put a fucking blood clot in his neck. A few of his shirt buttons were missing. Yates couldn't see a tear, but it was more likely the shirt that ripped than the denim. He braced himself, held his breath, and looked at Dylan's jeans. Specifically, the crotch of his jeans. He flared his nostrils at the undone top button but found relief in the fact Dylan's belt was still fastened. The creep in the alley couldn't have got his hand in Dylan's boxers. Yates released his breath and unclenched his fists. Two kicks to the ribs hadn't been enough.

"The en-suite is through there."

Dylan didn't reply.

"Hey." Yates grabbed Dylan by the ankle and shook him. His shoe popped off and clattered on the floor. Dylan released a blissful sigh and wriggled his toes, so Yates took off his other shoe too.

"Dylan. If you need to piss or be sick, the bathroom's the door on the right."

Dylan rolled onto his side. "Right."

"Don't go in the door on the left, understand?"

"Left. Understand."

Yates fidgeted at the end of the bed. He opened his mouth, but no words came out. He stood there gawping, picking his nails, waiting for something, but he didn't know what. *Did he wait to be dismissed?* He frowned. It was his goddamn house.

"Can you turn the light out?" Dylan mumbled.

He turned off the light but kept the door to the hallway open. If Dylan needed him, he only had to shout. Yates locked the front door, switched off the lights, then checked on Dylan one last time.

It wasn't until he was staring at the ceiling in the guest room that he questioned why he hadn't put Dylan in there instead. Sure, the bed wasn't as big and squishy, and the en-suite attached to the spare room only had a sink and a toilet, but why did Dylan need a big and squishy bed and a luxury bathroom?

Why had he put Dylan in his bed, and why did knowing he was in there feel good?

Why had he changed the sheets before he went out?

Yates rolled onto his side and refused to think any more about Dylan.

****

A retch pulled Yates from his sleep. He took a moment, confused why he was lying in a different direction, before remembering he was in the spare room and Dylan was in his king-size bed.

Oh.

"Fuck it." Yates pulled on his sweatpants and rushed down the corridor. He froze in the doorway. Dylan was gone from the bed, and a retch followed by a garbled sound came from the bathroom. He'd successfully thrown up in the toilet. The second time at least. The first load of sick dripped down the bedroom wall, filling the room with a putrid smell.

The toilet splashed and pattered. Dylan retched again.

"Christ," Yates muttered, pushing into the bathroom.

Dylan was halfway down the toilet bowl when Yates pulled him back.

He gripped onto Dylan's shoulders. "Get it all out."

"That's what I'm trying to do."

Yates snorted. Again, he'd said something stupid. It wasn't as if keeping it all in was an option in the first place. Dylan rested his chin on the toilet bowl and breathed hard through his nose.

"Where am I?"

"My house," Yates said. "15 Stonebridge, Barton, to be exact. I found you getting molested down an alley."

"Molested?"

"You were wasted and being taken advantage of."

"But was he hot, though?"

Yates gritted his teeth. He flashed a look at the toilet seat and thought about slamming it down on Dylan's head.

"That's not funny."

"I know," he whispered. "I'm sorry."

Dylan leaned back and turned his head. He frowned at Yates.

"You're the flower shop man?"

"Who did you think I was?"

He dropped his chin back to the toilet. "I don't know, someone, being nice."

"I'm not nice."

"You rescued me from a molester."

"I wanted to beat up the molester; you were baggage."

"I'll leave then." He attempted to stand, but Yates pinned him down by the shoulders.

"You're not going anywhere."

"Bossed around by the flower shop man."

Yates stared at the back of Dylan's head. "Why do you call me that?"

"Do you prefer florist?"

"No." Yates shook his head. "You know what I am; you know what I do."

"You sell flowers."

"And?"

Dylan tipped his head back again, looking dazed. "And what?"

"I kill people, not to mention this…" He kept hold of Dylan with one hand and gestured to his face with the other. Dylan's eyes fluttered shut, and he groaned, pressing his cheek on the toilet.

"My head…"

"Did you get sick on yourself?"

"No, I managed to hold it all in and get to the bathroom."

The bedroom wall said differently.

"I'll get you some water. Try not to drown yourself before I'm back." He smiled toothily. "I'd quite like to watch."

Dylan's laugh quickly turned into a groan.

Yates released him and hurried away. He grabbed a glass of water, an icepack, and one of his T-shirts in case Dylan had splashed-back vomit on his clothes.

When he returned to the bathroom, Dylan had crawled across the room and sat with his back against the bath. He blinked blearily at Yates as he pointed to his chest.

"That's a nice shirt."

Yates looked down at himself. "I'm not wearing a shirt. They're tattoos."

"You're covered."

Skulls, wolves, guns, trees. All skillfully inked. All realistic in style. All ruined by patches of rough, tight skin where the fire had burned him. Yates stiffened, waiting for Dylan to ask, but instead, he kept studying the tattoos while tilting his head. His eyes rolled, he fell to the side, and Yates pulled him upright.

"I think I like the dogs the best."

Yates glared. "They're wolves. Big, vicious, tear-your-throat-out wolves."

"They look cute."

"No, they don't. Drink this."

Dylan downed the lot and handed the glass back to Yates with a hint of a smile.

"Lean forward and put the ice pack on the back of your neck."

"The back of my neck?"

"Trust me."

Dylan leaned his head down and slapped the ice pack on his neck. He hissed, then hummed as the ice worked its magic and branched out its coldness.

"What did you take?"

"I don't know."

"So that arsehole in the alley could've roofied you?"

Dylan flashed Yates a guilty look. "I took it. He was there, but I chose to take it."

"Describe it."

"Circular pink pill. I think it had a z etched in the front."

"Do you take drugs often?"

"It was my first time; I didn't know what I was doing. I was just…"

Yates folded his arms and shifted to block the light on Dylan. "Upset over your ex?"

Dylan stopped wincing and looked up. "Don't call him that."

"So, he's not your ex?"

Dylan didn't answer.

"You're young—"

"So, I don't know what love is?"

Yates flexed his jaw, inwardly counted to ten, then started again. "You're young; you've got plenty of time to find someone to love, someone who wants to love you back, someone who does without even thinking about it."

"He does love me; it's complicated, that's all."

"Did you speak to your friends about it or your sister?"

Dylan drew his knees up to his chest. "They won't want to know."

"They care about you?"

"Yeah."

"Then they'll want to know. They'll want to help."

"He was my first."

"That doesn't mean he'll be your last."

"But he's the only guy I've…I've been intimate with."

"The sex that good, huh?"

Dylan narrowed his eyes and hissed away from Yates. "It's not about sex."

"So, the sex sucked."

"You're a robot, remember? You wouldn't understand."

"Are you trying to hurt my feelings?" He crouched down, face to face with Dylan. "You'll have to try a lot harder than that."

"Fine, I will."

Yates craned his neck closer and clutched the bath on either side of Dylan's head.

"And?"

Dylan's eyes whipped across Yates's scars. One on his chin, one on his cheek, and one on his forehead that twisted his eyebrow into an odd position. He waited for Dylan to draw attention to them, to sneer, and spit his disgust, and leaned in until they were almost nose to nose.

"Fiona Florist do better flowers than you."

Ouch. Yates drew back. Dylan's eyebrows flexed, and he lifted his chin, all smug and pleased in the face of a predator. Yates lowered his shoulders and stopped trapping Dylan against the bath.

He ruffled Dylan's hair and laughed. It sounded and felt odd. "Little bastard."

"It's true."

"It's not true."

Dylan nodded, still looking pleased. "They weren't open when you won that award. Next year, they're sure to beat you."

Yates stood up and towered over Dylan. "You seem to know rather a lot about Fiona Florist."

He shrugged. "I was in there a few weeks ago. They had a better color palette, more pastel shades, less bold block colors."

"I like bold colors—"

"But it's not about what you like, it's about what your customers like, and I was disappointed at your bouquets when I visited."

Yates looked away. An ugly heat built in his stomach. He tried to pin an emotion to it, not quite anger or rage; it was different. He shuffled, unable to look at Dylan. The sensation in his stomach threw him off. It fed up his body and blotched his cheeks.

"You only saw them for a few minutes. What the fuck do you know?"

"I saw them for longer than that, a few months ago now, but I remember."

"What?" Yates frowned down at him. "Last Saturday was the first time I've ever seen you."

"Maybe, but it wasn't the first time I've been in your shop. I was there, you were there, not my fault you didn't notice me. I noticed you."

"I'm pretty fucking hard to miss."

Yates stared at Dylan but couldn't place him in the shop. He'd had plenty of visitors after his shop had been announced best in the county, too many faces to remember.

"Who were you with?"

"My sister."

Still nothing.

Yates shook his head. "You're making this shit up. I would've remembered you."

"Why?"

"Pathetic faces seem to stick in my head, and yours is a perfect specimen. Come on, you can't sleep there."

He held his hand out, and after a few attempts, Dylan managed to grip on. Yates lifted him carefully to his feet, swung Dylan's arm over his shoulder, and hobbled out from the bathroom.

Dylan came to a halt by the sicked-on wall. "Did you do that?"

"Like hell did I do that!"

"Well, it wasn't me!"

Yates dragged him out of the room while muttering curses under his breath.

He lowered Dylan onto the spare bed and told him to stay put while he sorted out the bathroom and the bedroom wall. By the time he'd finished, Dylan was breathing softly, lying diagonally across the mattress.

"Little bastard."

It was a choice between his bed in a room that reeked of sick or the cold leather sofa in the living room. He chose the sofa and huffed at the ceiling as he tried to get comfortable.

Fiona Florist did not do better flowers than him, but he would be visiting them to see why Dylan thought so, in Cognito, of course.

****

Yates's eyes flew open at the sound of a curse. A shouted curse. He rolled over and crashed to his knees before looking up. Living room, his addled mind supplied. Dylan's shout had come from upstairs, and Yates rushed towards the sound.

He wasn't in the spare room but in the master bedroom, wide-eyed and edging further away from Yates along the wall.

"What is it?"

Dylan darted a look at the left door.

"Did you go in there?"

"Is that where you kill people?"

The closet was full of costumes, swings, restraints, whips. It wasn't a psychopath's lair with blood, hooks, and chainsaws all over the walls.

"They're sex toys."

"But there's a body in there."

"Huh?" Yates strode past him and thrust open the door. He could see why, in certain lighting, Dylan thought there was a body crushed into the back corner.

"It's a sex doll."

"A sex doll?"

Yates stepped inside and hauled it up. Not a cheap blow-up doll, but a sex robot. One of its eyes was half shut, and half of its mouth was pulled up in a smile. It'd cost a fortune and was a gift for Ranger in case he couldn't find a boyfriend.

"It's a guy, not a girl?"

Yates put it back on the floor.

"Do you want something to eat?"

Dylan shook his head. "No, I'd better be going… Thank you for letting me crash here. I hope I wasn't too much trouble."

"No, not too much, just the sick on the wall, the insult, and accusing me of storing dead bodies in my closet."

"When did I insult you?"

Yates turned around. "You said Fiona Florist was better."

Dylan squeezed his temples. "Oh yeah, I did."

When Dylan didn't apologize or retract his opinion, Yates huffed and pointed to the bedroom door. "Time for you to leave. There's a bus stop up the road."

"Thank you." Dylan slipped out the door while scratching his head. He darted looks back at Yates stalking behind him. When they got to the front door, Yates ordered him to stop, and he did, nipping his lip with worry, Yates left him on the doormat and disappeared into the kitchen.

He returned with a cool bottle of water from the fridge and three cereal bars. "Take these."

Dylan smiled. "Thanks—"

"And take this too."

Dylan frowned at the box and ran his fingers over the gold letters. The annihilator.

"The annihilator?"

"Something for you to have a little fun with later and distract you from your ex-boyfriend blues."

Dylan ran his fingers lightly over the letters again, barely grazing them with his fingertips. Yates's cock tingled, and he tried not to imagine his cock as the box, Dylan's eyes wide with fascination as he took it in.

"Whatever it is, it's big and heavy."

It was no use; he was growing harder watching Dylan handle the annihilator box.

Dylan froze. His eyebrows slammed down, and he squinted at Yates.

"It's not a sex toy, is it?"

"Yes."

His cheeks reddened, and he tried to give it back, but Yates kept his arms by his sides, refusing to take it.

"I can't have this."

"Why not?"

"I don't know what to do with it."

"It'll become quite straightforward when you get it out. After all, you owe me," Yates said, lifting his eyebrows.

"What?"

"I took you home last night, and now you owe me. Give it a go, at least once. That's all I'm asking."

Dylan licked his lips and weighed the box with his hand. "What if I don't like it?"

"Stop using it, but swing by Blooming Bloomers and let me know. It's supposed to be a guaranteed prostate orgasm."

Dylan's whole face glowed red.

"Now, get lost."

He pushed Dylan's chest, gently so as not to tip him over, and Dylan took a step back out of the house. Before Dylan could speak, Yates closed the door on him and rested his forehead against it. Dylan hadn't noticed the tented erection in Yates's pants, but it was insistent in its twitching and jerking.

It needed dealing with, and fast.

CHAPTER FIVE

Yates closed his eyes to fight off motion sickness. It didn't help. "Hold it goddamn still."

"I am," Ranger hissed.

He directed his phone at the bouquet. They were pastel shades like Dylan had described, and as much as it pained Yates to admit it, the arrangement was spot on. Blue hydrangeas, blush pink roses, and lilac carnations. Soft and pleasing on the eye, no doubt they smelled good too.

"Show me more."

"Okay," Ranger whispered. Yates looked away from the whirling camera. "What about these?"

Coral roses, pink lilies, and sprigs of orange asclepias. Yates punched the counter, gritting his teeth.

"They're fucking beautiful."

A tear burned his eye.

Ranger snorted. "Wait until you see the roses…"

"They better not be bigger than mine."

Supersized red roses filled the screen.

"Fuck."

"The label says they come with a box of chocolates and a bottle of champagne too."

"Is it busy in there?"

Ranger lifted the phone and showed Yates the customers.

"Don't make it obvious."

"Do this, do that," Ranger huffed. "Don't do this, don't do that—"

"Can I help you?"

The camera stayed on the flowers, but Yates heard the sickly-sweet voice followed by Ranger's reply. "I'm just browsing…"

"Spying," Yates corrected in Ranger's ear.

"Actually," Ranger said, "what would you suggest for a first date?"

"Don't you dare conspire with the enemy—"

The woman chuckled. "An orchid is always a good choice."

"If you buy an orchid from her, I swear I'll push it up your arse...roots first."

"Here let me show you some. We have a variety of colors."

"They're stunning," Ranger said. "Best I've seen in the whole county."

"Fuck the roots, I'll start with the flowerpot, and I'll insert it eye-wateringly slowly." Yates tipped his head back and groaned to the ceiling. "Orchids? What year is this woman from?"

"I'd say the sixties."

"Sorry, what?"

Ranger laughed. "Nothing, talking aloud, that's all."

Even the orchids were sublime. So perfect they looked fake. Yates glared at his award on the shelf, as good as gone.

"Are you Fiona?" Ranger asked.

"Yes, Fiona, the florist of *Fiona Florist*."

She laughed, and Ranger did too.

"Fucking spare me," Yates grumbled.

Yates could only see a section of Fiona's shirt, but that was enough to make him want to hurl something. She wore a daisy pattern. He had a shirt with an identical pattern in his closet at home.

"How are you settling in?" Ranger asked.

"Business is booming, or blooming, should I say."

Ha, fucking ha.

Yates glanced to the office. He had a gun in his desk, ready to blow his brains out if Fiona said any more godawful puns.

"I usually buy my flowers from Blooming Bloomers."

"Never heard of it."

Yates cracked his knuckles. *Bitch.*

"The guy that owns it is a grump."

"You're never coming in here again."

Ranger went on. "But the flowers are good."

"Too fucking right they're good. Award. Winning."

Fiona chuckled again. "I might have to visit and have a nosey around."

"If her nose comes in here, I'm chopping it off."

The bell to the shop sounded, and Yates glanced over to see Dylan heading towards him. He watched him approach, skittish like an animal ready to bolt.

A few days had passed since Yates had pushed him through his front door, and each night, he ended up jerking off over him. He sighed and put his phone down on the counter; Ranger's camera was still aimed at the orchids in every color.

A rainbow display. Fiona began picking up individual pots to show him. Ranger oohed and awwed to piss Yates off, but like a car crash, he couldn't stop glancing at the wreckage.

He flicked his eyes toward Dylan. "Come to look at my below-par flowers?"

"No."

"Then you've got feedback from the annihilator."

Dylan tripped a few meters from Yates. "I...I haven't used it yet."

"Why not?"

He shrugged and scratched the back of his head.

"You're not back with your ex, are you?"

"Stop calling him that, and no."

Yates folded his arms. "Then why come in my shop?"

Dylan swung his rucksack off his back. "It's so dead in here I thought it would be the perfect place to study."

"It's Wednesday at two. It isn't one of my peak days or my peak hours."

"And when's your peak days and hours?"

Valentine's Day morning. Mother's Day afternoon.

"Ah, shit!"

Yates dropped his gaze to the phone on the counter. Ranger spun around, the colors of the shop all blended. Fiona yelled something Yates didn't catch.

"Abort, abort!"

"Ranger?"

"I've been rumbled."

Ranger's feet boomed along a pavement. Yates caught a glimpse of the sky, a shop, a car that came close to knocking Ranger down, a barking dog, then more pavement.

"What happened?"

"I heard you asking about an annihilator and asked to see it. She saw my earpiece."

Dylan inched closer with his attention locked on the phone. "Is he all right?"

"He's being his normal self."

Ranger clattered into a car, rolling over the top and landing on his feet.

"What happened?" Dylan asked.

"I sent a man undercover. Looks like he blew it."

"Yates—"

He cut Ranger off mid-yelp and dropped his phone on the counter.

"Shouldn't you go help him?"

"No. He threatened to buy her orchid."

"What?"

"Never mind, he'll be fine." Yates waved Dylan's confusion away. "Why do you need to study? You're a drama student, isn't it all scripts and stages?"

"There's coursework too, drama in context, playwriting—wait. How did you know I studied drama?"

"I saw your books in your rucksack."

"Makes sense." Dylan rocked forward on his toes. "So can I?"

"Can you what?"

"Study here?"

Yates blinked at him. "Don't you have a room?"

"I do, but my housemates both do music. It's not a peaceful environment to study."

"A classroom? The library? A fucking morgue? Are those places not peaceful enough?"

Dylan cleared a space for his rucksack and started unloading his books. "Can you believe it? The morgue had more life than this place."

"Just this once," Yates said as he went to fetch his chair from the office. He slid it over to Dylan, who gave him a big grin.

"Thank you."

"Literally, don't mention it."

Just this once.

****

No matter how many times Yates sneered and groaned, Dylan kept coming back, kept waiting until Yates gave up his chair. In the end, Yates bought a new chair, which brightened Dylan's face with victory. He had gained a permanent place in the shop, much to Yates's fury, but he didn't growl at him to leave or threaten to throw him out the window. He allowed it.

"How come freckles gets a chair?" Ranger asked, not so subtly, at the top of his voice.

"Dylan's using my old chair—"

"But you only bought it a few months back."

Yates's face reddened. "Was there something you wanted?"

"Some advice."

"About?"

"My profile picture."

Ranger turned his phone towards Yates. "Do I go for the topless gym picture?"

Yates cursed at the picture of Ranger grinning like an idiot. "Or?"

"The cute animal lover."

He scrolled to the next picture, him still shirtless but holding two kittens and pulling an even more ridiculous face.

"What the actual fuck?"

"What? I love animals."

Yates lifted his eyebrow. "Really?"

"Yes, really."

"You know, I had a budgie once."

Ranger held out his arms. "I love birds—"

"You shot it because it was too loud."

"What?" Ranger floundered, lost for a moment.

Yates took his phone and snapped a picture. "Now that's the perfect one."

"I didn't kill a bird."

"You kill people all the time, but killing a bird is somehow worse?"

Ranger darted a look back at Dylan, who tried his hardest not to laugh. "You do know freckles can hear you?"

"I know, and he's called Dylan."

Dylan waved. "Hi."

Ranger frowned, then turned back to Yates. "Right… I'm confused."

"Doesn't take much." Yates sighed. "He knows, and it's his choice to be here, so I guess it doesn't bother him so much."

"Right…So which picture?" Ranger asked.

"Neither. They're both hideous."

"Try looking in a mirror."

Dylan pushed off from his chair. "Let me see them."

Ranger did, but he narrowed his eyes in suspicion. "And?"

"I don't like either of them."

Yates puffed out his chest. "See. It wasn't just me being an arsehole."

"You need to look more casual," Dylan said. He pulled Ranger away from Yates, towards the flowers. "Like here, just smile."

"Got it."

Ranger smiled but tensed both his arms in a strong man pose.

"Erm…lose the arms."

"Really?"

Dylan nodded.

"Okay, how about…" Ranger curled his fingers into the bottom of his vest and made a move to lift it.

"No!"

"No?" Ranger lifted his eyebrow. "I've got a hot body."

"Maybe that'll be a nice thing to discover…rather than seeing it straight away. Clothes stay on."

"Okay, I'm gonna trust you, Dylan." Ranger spun around and grabbed a rose.

"Goddamn it, Ranger," Yates growled.

Dylan shook his head. "Lose the rose."

Ranger flung it over his shoulder. "Done."

"I swear, you're gonna go through the window."

"Now smile," Dylan said, "but not too much, a small smile."

"A minimal amount of teeth," Ranger nodded. "I've been practicing."

"Practicing?" Yates asked.

"Smiling in the mirror. You should try it. Your smile could strip flesh from bone."

Dylan laughed, casting a quick look over at Yates. He didn't smile. He pressed his lips in an angry line.

"I think I've hit my *Ranger* limit for today."

"There ya go," Dylan said, handing the phone back to Ranger.

He checked the picture and nodded. "I'd do me. Would you?"

Dylan blinked. "Huh?"

"Or more accurately, would you let me do you?"

"You're…you're not my type."

"But Yates is, right?"

Yates's heart stopped in his chest. Dylan inched closer to the door, ready to bolt.

"Ranger, out," Yates growled.

"I only wondered."

"Out!"

He threw up his hands as he retreated. "I'm off. Later, bitches."

"Bitches?" Dylan whispered.

"Yup."

Ranger slipped through the front door, leaving Dylan and Yates to glance awkward looks at each other.

"So it's lunchtime," Yates said, inwardly cursing himself. What a stupid thing to say. *Yet again.* He sighed, grabbing his sandwich box from beneath the counter. He stiffened at the screech of chair legs. Dylan pushed his chair up to the counter and sat down with his lunch in his lap.

Yates swallowed at the new development.

"Your friend seems nice."

"Nice isn't the word I'd use to describe him."

Dylan lowered his gaze. "He's an assassin too?"

"Yes. A very good one."

"Does that mean you're a bad one?"

Yates snorted. "No. Just an inactive one."

"Inactive?"

"I've not done a hit myself in quite a while."

"Conscience finally caught up with you?"

"No. I'm waiting for the right arsehole to kill. He's being particularly evasive."

Dylan picked at his sandwich. "Does…does he deserve it?"

Yates tilted his head. "Yes. He does."

He didn't elaborate, and Dylan didn't press. He picked up his sandwich and took a bite. They ate in silence, all until Yates got out a bag of crisps. Dylan's face lit up, and he reached for one. "My favorite."

"I don't think so." Yates slid the packet away.

"Come on, don't be cruel."

"Buy your own."

"I'm a poor student."

Yates crunched a chip between his teeth. "So?"

Dylan smiled and launched across the counter. Yates blocked his attempt with ease and sent Dylan hurtling back. He crashed to the floor.

"Shit."

Yates rushed around to help him up. Dylan wobbled, rubbing the back of his head.

"Okay?"

"Yeah, fine." Dylan grinned and snatched the bag of crisps off the counter. "I win!"

"You're such a little shit."

He said it with a sigh, and his gut plummeted. He'd sounded like Donnie when he spoke about Elliot.

****

The bell on the door rang, and Yates looked up expecting Ranger, but Adam came up to the counter with a glum expression plastered to his face.

Yates cleared his tightening throat. "Is Edna…"

"She's still alive. The doctors were hopeful she'd be able to go home soon, but she got an infection after the surgery."

"Shit."

"It's been touch and go. Fevers and delirium. She kept asking for you, though. That's why I'm here. Will you visit her?"

"Of course."

"Whenever you're free."

"Right now." Yates snapped his fingers, and Dylan looked over. "I need you to go."

"What? Why?"

"Don't ask me what or why. Out."

Dylan shoved his books back into his rucksack and followed Adam out of the shop. Yates checked his emails one last time before locking up. Adam had already gone, but Dylan waited outside, clutching the strap of his rucksack so hard his knuckles had turned white.

"Has something happened?"

"My friend in the hospital is staying ill just to get my attention."

"So you lock up everything and close for the day?"

Yates turned to him. "Yes. I do."

"And you say you don't care about anyone…"

The soft smile said it was a gentle tease, but all it did was raise Yates's hackles. He crowed Dylan into the side of the shop.

"She's a customer. Not that it's any of your business."

He moved away from Dylan, but he snagged Yates's arm and tugged him. "I'm sorry, I didn't mean to pry."

Yates glared at the hands around his arm, Dylan had used both to grab him, and even together they barely stretched around his bicep. He swallowed down the rest of his anger and looked at Dylan's twitchy face. His eyes were round, his eyebrow jerked, and without thinking he touched Dylan's hair. It dissolved his lingering unease, and Dylan relaxed his shoulders in time with his long sigh.

"I shouldn't have snapped."

It was the closest thing to an apology Dylan was ever going to get.

"That's okay. I shouldn't have asked. I was curious, that's all. You looked…concerned."

"You must have been mistaken."

"Yeah, must've been." Dylan shot him a smile. "Can I come study in the shop tomorrow?"

"If you've got nowhere else, and I mean, nowhere else."

The skin around Dylan's eyes crinkled with a knowing smile. He knew Yates liked having him in the shop, and it infuriated Yates that he was so transparent. If Dylan was in the shop, it meant he wasn't somewhere else getting molested or walking a thin line between life and death.

"Now get out of here before I…"

"Before you what?"

A car whizzed past.

"Throw you into traffic."

Dylan just smiled, squeezed Yates's bicep then backed off. It was only when Dylan stepped away that Yates realized he'd been brushing his fingers through Dylan's hair the entire time.

Idle hands.

He needed to arrange another night with Darius as soon as he could.

****

"I hear you got an infection just to get my attention."

Edna didn't reply. Her eyes were shut, her breathing even. Yates sat down beside her and took her hand. She startled awake and attempted to slap him.

"Calm down, grandma."

He caught her swaying hand and lowered it to her chest.

"Yates?"

"I came to visit. The wonderful Adam dropped by and told me you were sick…sicker."

Edna swallowed. "He didn't try to get any more flowers off you, did he?"

"No, he seemed sad."

"He was in here yesterday, and I swear he was sizing me up for a coffin."

"You make sure you get the most expensive one you can find in existence. Gold plated, with diamonds, on a horse-drawn carriage. Go out with a bang."

"Out with a bang? I'll get launched from a canon then."

Yates smiled, but it didn't last long. He followed the tubes going into Edna's thin arms. She'd lost weight, most noticeably in her face. Each time she breathed, her cheeks sucked in.

"If I'd have known you were coming, I would've put some makeup on."

"That would've made me self-conscious."

"Actually…the bedside cabinet next to you, top drawer."

Yates stuck his hand inside, pushing past Edna's purse and a tub of moisturizer. "What am I looking for?"

"Nail varnish."

He slammed the drawer shut. "I'm not doing your nails."

"You're an evil man."

"The worst." He gestured to the white patches stuck to Edna's arms and legs. "What are these?"

"Ice packs to cool my temperature," Edna said. "My fever has been coming and going. They've been messing with my dreams."

"How?"

"One minute it's snowy Alaska, the next minute it's Hawaii."

"Sounds nice."

"The thing is, I've not been to either place."

Yates touched one of the patches.

"Can you lean forward?"

"Of course, I can…just about."

Yates encouraged her up and slid an icepack behind her neck. Edna lay back down. Her eyes fluttered, and she breathed out.

"That's surprisingly nice."

"When I was a kid, our freezer was stocked with ice packs."

"Why?"

"My mum used to get a lot of headaches."

From drinking far too much.

"Did you look after her?" Edna asked.

"For as long as I could stand it. Apart from the fever, how are you feeling?"

"Like I don't have long left."

"Edna…"

"No." She put her hand onto Yates's. "I don't want to talk about it. I don't want to talk about me or anything to do with me. I want you to talk, and I'll listen."

"That's a first."

"Arsehole."

Yates looked away. "How's the food in here?"

"But not about the bloody food."

"I'm no good at talking. I prefer to listen, judge, and be an arsehole. That's me."

Edna peeked a look at him, then closed her eyes. "Fine, I'll ask questions and you answer, that easier?"

"Which one of these buttons does the morphine? I think you could do with a top-up."

"Did you try the annihilator?"

Yates laughed and leaned closer. "You really want to be talking about that kinda thing here?"

"It's all doom and gloom. I need something fun. So…how fun was it?"

"I gave it away."

"To who?"

"Someone who needed it more."

Edna turned her head towards him. "Explain."

"When I visited you last, there was a guy on the roof of the hospital threatening to jump. Well, he says he wasn't going to jump, but he was rather close to the edge. It was a cry for help. He's going through a painful breakup."

"So you thought a vibrator would answer his prayers?"

"The vibrator wasn't my first option. I tried to get him to talk to someone at the hospital, encouraged him to confide in his friends and family, but he seems to have…"

"Have what?"

"Decided to cling to me."

"God help him."

Yates snorted. "He's been coming to the shop for a few weeks now."

"And does what?"

"He studies. Drama. He's in his second year. I cleared him a space in the shop, and he comes in every few days, sits and studies until I close up at six."

"Do you keep the space clear for him every day?"

"Yeah, I never know what day he'll be there—"

She chuckled softly.

Yates flared his nostrils. "What is it, Wicked Witch of the West?"

"Nothing, nothing at all. Describe him to me." Edna tapped her temple. "I can't picture him."

"Messy black hair, freckles, brown eyes, slim, short. Young. Pathetic expression. Big eyebrows, thin lips."

"You want to fuck him?"

Yates deflated and held on to his head. "Like you can't possibly believe."

Edna chuckled. "But he's straight?"

"No, he's not."

"What's the but?"

Yates glared at her, but it had no effect with her eyes shut.

"He doesn't need fucking; he needs someone to talk to."

"You're the one who gave him the annihilator, remember?"

Yates grunted and fell back in his chair. "I thought it would loosen him up."

Edna quirked her eyebrows. "I bet you did."

"You and your dirty mind."

"Don't tell me you haven't imagined him using it."

Of course, he had.

Yates shifted in his seat and refused to answer.

"Just fuck him, Yates. Life is too short."

"No. He's too fragile for me."

Edna's jaw dropped. Yates glared at her gawping until it went on for too long. He shoved her arm, and her jaw snapped shut.

"Don't do that. I thought you'd died."

"I very nearly did. You care about someone other than yourself. That is heart-stopping."

"I don't care. I just don't want to fuck him up any more than he is already. If something happens to him, I don't want to feel responsible for being part of it. I've killed enough people on purpose; I don't want to kill this one by accident."

"This guy has got under your skin, hasn't he?"

No. He's nothing. No one.

Words blurted from Yates before he could stop them.

"It feels like he's putting his life in my hands, and I don't know what to do with it. I keep trying to pass him off to someone else, *anyone* else, but he won't go."

His heart thumped faster. *Why was it thumping faster?* Yates pressed his palm against it, frowning.

Edna's eyes peeled open. She grinned at him.

"I'm glad I was alive to see this."

"See what?"

"You blushing."

He wasn't. He knew he wasn't. But he checked his face in the camera of his phone.

"I think you're having one of your delirious spells again."

"What's his name?"

"Right, I'm getting the doctor."

"Please don't. He's irritatingly optimistic."

"Nothing like hoping for the best."

"But preparing for the worst." She squeezed his hand. "It's okay, you know."

"What is?"

"This." When she moved her arm, the tubes shook. "I told you before, all things considered, I've had a good life."

"And I told you before, it's still going." He leaned in and whispered in her ear. "It could get even better, all you've got to do is hang in there, and you'll find out."

"Bring every flower to my funeral, one of each."

Yates threw himself back. "Christ, Edna."

"Promise."

"I promise."

"And the young guy with the messy black hair and freckles."

"Dylan?"

Edna gave him her most devious grin. "So that's his name."

"Sly, old fox."

"Bring him." She nodded. "I want to meet him, but not when I'm here, not when I'm not my best."

"No, he'll get to meet you for the split second you fly past us from the canon."

Edna laughed. "As long as you're there with him, I'll have a smile on my face."

"Daft woman."

"Dirty dog."

Yates grunted and yanked open the top drawer of the bedside cabinet.

Edna drifted off during the second coat of yellow nail varnish. Yates stayed to do a third.

CHAPTER SIX

Yates spotted Dylan racing down the street. His black hair bobbing up and down with each stride, cheeks red and round. He skidded to a stop in front of Yates and grabbed him by the collar of his shirt.

"I need your help!"

Yates pulled Dylan behind him and assessed the street. The cars passing travelled at normal speed. No faces had been drawn towards them. Still, he waited for an assailant to launch at Dylan. His clenched fists shook. His bent knees began to ache. Whoever was after Dylan would be eating the curb and choking on their spleen soon enough.

Yates spun around at the tap to his shoulder.

"What?"

Dylan beat his back, but in Yates's pumped-up state, he barely felt it.

"You're crushing me against the wall."

"You said you needed help."

Yates gave him some room and waited for Dylan's explanation. He leaned forward and panted at the pavement. After twenty seconds, Yates had hit the limit of his patience.

"Spit it out, will you! I've got somewhere to be. If you're not in trouble…"

Dylan held up his forefinger, a gesture to wait while he caught his breath. Yates stared at his finger, anyone else's, and he would've reached over and snapped it.

"I'm in trouble."

Yates stiffened and checked the pavements, the roads, the windows, the roofs. Unless Dylan was being pursued by the invisible man, there was no one there.

"What kind of trouble?"

"The sister kind."

Sister?

Yates stepped back. The adrenaline puffing him up like a blowfish ebbed away. "I can't help you with that."

"Yes, you can."

He turned away. "I'm going."

"Please." Dylan dropped to his knees and shuffled forward. He gripped onto Yates's thighs and pleaded with huge, glistening eyes. "I really need you."

Yates looked away and pinched the bridge of his nose. It was like the start of one of his fantasies. Dylan blowing him in full view of everyone in the doorway of his shop.

His sex-starved mind ran riot.

"Yates."

The zipper on his jeans began to burn.

"Dylan."

He pressed closer, his chin touched Yates's groin, and he stepped back, only for Dylan to shift closer on his knees and bring his chin in contact with Yates's crotch again.

"Please, Yates, I'll do anything."

It was too much. He was seconds away from unzipping himself and giving Dylan the *anything* he'd offered to do.

Yates leaned down, hooked Dylan under the shoulders, and hauled him to his feet. "It's a terrible idea to say things like that to me."

"But I mean it."

"No, you don't."

"Try me."

Yates spun away. "Why are we even having this conversation? I can't help you with your sister."

"How do you know?"

"I don't have one for a start."

Dylan grabbed his hand when he went to walk away. "You haven't even heard what the problem is."

"I don't care what it is. I care about getting home. Eating something, showering, and waiting for eight o'clock."

"What happens at eight o'clock?"

"None of your goddamn business."

Yates looked up the road, but his feet wouldn't follow. In two hours, he'd be fist-deep in Darius. He needed it. He didn't need Dylan tempting him and pulling him deeper into a responsibility he didn't want.

Dylan locked their fingers together.

"It's my sister's hen do tonight, at least she thinks it is. The maid of honor got ill, so I stepped in, said I'd arrange it, except with everything else going on, I didn't."

Dylan's voice trembled. Yates closed his eyes and inwardly chanted, "Don't look at him," over and over.

"She's going to hate me."

"She won't if you tell her what's been going on."

"Please, Yates, you've got to help me."

Don't look at him.

He pulled his hand free from Dylan's grip. "I don't have to do anything."

"Please."

The heartstring in Yates's chest twanged.

Motherfucker.

He couldn't help himself. He looked. At some point, Dylan had dropped back to his knees again. Tears clung to his lashes; one shone on his chin. His eyebrows twitched, his lips shook. Without a doubt, he looked more tragic than hot, but Yates's cock still took an interest.

His heart picked up the pace in his chest, strumming his one remaining heartstring.

"How the hell am I any help?"

Dylan got to his feet and flung himself at Yates. He hugged him tightly. The motion set loose the tears from his lashes. Yates followed one with his thumb as it fell. He marveled at Dylan's silk soft skin and imagined his cum dripping down it.

No, that wasn't helpful. He mustn't have those thoughts.

"Your shop."

"My shop?"

"Maybe…maybe we can do something."

"You want to throw the hen party in my shop?"

"Of course I don't want to, but I don't know what else to do."

Yates flexed his jaw. "Why not ask Fiona from Fiona Florist?"

"They were booked tonight."

"Get off me."

Dylan hugged him tighter. His wet cheek soaked through the fabric of Yates's shirt.

"Sorry, it was a joke, a badly timed joke. Hannah's really excited. I didn't know what to say to her. I panicked and told her and her friends to meet me here."

"What the hell, Dylan?"

"I know, I'm sorry."

"Flower arranging is hardly a hen-do activity."

"With lots of alcohol, anything is a hen-do activity."

"I don't have lots of alcohol."

"I'll get some. Will you help me? I don't have a clue what to do, and I'm cracking up here. I've fucked up big time, I—"

"Shush." Yates pressed his finger against Dylan's lips. "Your panic is annoying."

And a turn-on.

His lips were warm and wet from a tear that slid over them. Fuck, it was getting more and more tempting for Yates to taste his desperation. Kiss it from his eyes, lick it from his cheeks, suck it from lips.

"I'm sorry I—"

Yates tapped his finger against Dylan's lips. "I told you to shush."

Dylan nodded.

"I'll help you, okay?"

Dylan collapsed into him, forcing his lips into Yates's finger. They were thin but spongy, soft. Very kissable. They drew Yates's eyes and kept them there.

Stop thinking about his mouth.

He removed his finger and leaned down with his gaze locked on Dylan's lips. "But for a price."

He was an arsehole. A sex-starved one.

"How much?" Dylan asked, untangling himself from Yates. He swung his rucksack off his back. "I haven't paid my student loan back into the bank yet."

"Not that kind of price. You said you'd do anything."

Dylan swallowed. "Anything."

Let me fuck you. Let me blow you. Let me tie you up and come all over your face. The options were endless. The fantasies stretched before him. It left his head woozy with the prospect.

"Yates?"

He snapped back to the present. "Come to my place tomorrow night."

"Okay," Dylan whispered.

No fight, no anger, but a barely audible okay.

"And bring the annihilator with you."

"Why?"

Yates licked his lips. "I'm gonna teach you how to use it."

Dylan's lashes fluttered. He nodded as his face pinkened. "I'll bring it."

"That's tomorrow; right now, we need to salvage your sister's hen do."

****

Yates filled the office with as many premium plants and flowers as he could. He pushed back the display tables, clearing a space in the middle of the shop. Dylan sat on his usual chair, blowing up balloons as if his life depended on it.

The bell rang, and Yates waved in the delivery man.

Champagne box after champagne box. He'd never seen that much booze before. Yates snorted bitterly. Yeah, he had. Easily. But not champagne. Bottles, cans, and fucking kegs of beer.

The delivery man cleared his throat, and Yates slapped a wad of cash down in his palm. He scarpered, and Yates moved the boxes under the tables with his foot.

"We need chairs," Dylan said.

He panted and held a balloon so weakly the air leaked out before he could tie it.

"Have a rest before you pass out."

"Where the hell are we going to get chairs?"

Yates's eyes fixed on the bakery on the other side of the street. The lights were still on; he could see movement inside. The Bakery Boys. Four brothers who often took turns glaring at Yates across the street.

"I'm going to get us some."

"Wait…"

Yates glanced over his shoulder. "What is it?"

"Be nice."

"I'm not nice."

"Act nice then."

Yates released a long exhale through his nose. *Why was he doing this again?*

"Please," Dylan whispered.

That was why.

Yates made no promises and left the shop.

The blinds were down, but the lights were still on. Yates didn't bother knocking but strode straight into the bakery with his 'don't mess with me' expression plastered to his face. The bell cheerfully announced his entry, and a brother bulldozed through colorful tassels that acted as a door. His brow twitched, and he muttered curses under his breath, but they didn't appear to be directed at Yates.

"We're shut."

He came closer. Yates got a good look at his apron, splattered red. He looked more like a butcher than a chef.

"I'm not here for a cake or a damn sausage roll."

"What do you want?"

Yates dragged his gaze away from the red smears and up to Stone's hard eyes. The oldest brother and the one that ran the bakery. Yates actually preferred him, but splattered in blood, the sight of him lifted the hairs on the back of his neck.

"I need some of your chairs."

"Are you asking me for them, or telling me you're about to take them?"

"I'm asking."

Stone nodded. "£100 and they're yours for the night."

"What?"

"That's the deal. Take it or leave it."

Yates glanced across the road at Dylan puffing on a limp balloon, lungs too weak to finish. He prayed it wasn't a sign of things to come.

"Fine." He grabbed his wallet and cleared out the rest of his cash. "Am I supposed to ignore the blood on your apron?"

Stone sighed as he looked down at himself. "It's for the best."

"Next time, you might want to lock your door."

"It always slips my mind," Stone mused.

"Thanks for the chairs."

Yates pinned the door open with his foot and struggled through but paused on the threshold. He heard a shrill whimper from the back room. Stone's eyes burned into the back of his head.

"Anything else, Yates?"

"No, I think we're good."

"Wait..."

Stone moved from behind the counter, approaching Yates from behind. He stiffened as Stone reached over his shoulder and placed a brown paper bag on top of the chairs. "I don't want them to go to waste."

Stone stayed in the doorway with his glare fixed on Yates. Even once he was back inside the flower shop, he lingered.

"Were you nice?"

Yates dropped the chairs on the floor. "I've got some, haven't I?"

"I know, but you didn't...you know?"

Dylan shot a guilty look across the street to Stone, still glaring.

"No, I didn't threaten to kill anyone." He peeked inside the paper bag. "He even sent you a pink doughnut."

"Really?" Dylan smiled at stoic Stone and even gave him a wave. To Yates's surprise, Stone waved back before disappearing into the bakery.

"That wasn't blood on him, right?"

"Chocolate."

"Why is it red?"

Yates didn't answer. He left Stone to whatever it was he did, and Stone did the same to him.

"When your sister gets here, the shop's yours. Just don't break anything."

"What?"

Dylan let go of the balloon. It whizzed around the shop, showering Yates with spit. He gritted his teeth and inwardly counted to ten.

"Where will you be?"

"I'm going home." Yates checked his watch. Forty minutes until Darius knocked on his door. He still had time for a quick shower. He'd have to eat once he'd tied Darius up, but that would add to the kidnapped role play. Even kidnappers had to have a break to eat.

"I'll be back at two for the keys. I booked a striper for midnight. If he asks for money, don't give him any. He's already been paid."

"You can't go. What if...what if I burn down the shop?"

"I suggest you don't do that."

"Yates." Dylan sprung to his feet. He swayed and collapsed back down again.

"Take a minute. Just breathe, Dylan." Yates gripped his shoulder to steady him. "I said you should've quit it with the balloons."

"There's fifty in the pack."

"Doesn't mean you have to blow up every single one."

"You can't leave. Who's going to do the flower arranging demo?"

He waved his hand in the direction of the table of flowers he'd set up to be destroyed.

"You don't need a demo. Shove them together and voilà."

Dylan shook his head. "There's more to it than that."

That was true, but not to drunk women on a hen do.

"I've given you my shop, bought you booze, got you chairs, a stripper, a game of twister. What more do you want from me?"

Dylan grabbed the bottom of Yates's shirt. "I want you to stay."

"I'm not a people person."

"I've seen you putting it on when people come into the shop."

"That's for ten minutes at a time. And it's not for a load of intoxicated women. Not to mention"—he showed Dylan his watch—"I'm running late."

"What are you doing at eight o'clock?"

Lie, shout at him that it's none of his business. Both options went through Yates's head, but instead, he leaned close to Dylan's and spoke the truth.

"Fucking a guy. That's what I've got planned. He'll be knocking on my door at eight, and I'll be waiting. Now have a good night."

Dylan tightened his grip on Yates's shirt. He avoided eye contact and instead stared at Yates's chest. "You've got a boyfriend?"

"No. I've got an arrangement."

"You should have told me."

Yates glanced at the time. Only thirty minutes to get home. "Why?"

"Because you're gonna fuck him and fuck me the next day. I deserve to know that."

"Number one: I don't owe you an explanation, and number two: I'm not going to fuck you tomorrow."

No matter how badly he wanted to.

"But you said—"

"I said I'd teach you how to use the annihilator, and then I'm going to send you on your merry way."

"Cancel your date tonight."

"It's not a date."

Dylan looked up at him. "Cancel him, and whatever you were planning on doing with him, do with me instead tomorrow."

"You couldn't handle it."

"Try me."

He narrowed his eyes and attempted to glare Yates down. His defiant display only made Yates laugh, and he set about crushing Dylan's misplaced confidence.

"Darius has a pain kink and loves roleplaying."

"So?"

"I'm going to restrain him to my bed, push needles through his nipples, and he's going to beg for me to stop, but I won't."

Dylan drew back, but Yates wasn't done.

"I'm going to shove a dildo into him, so big your eyes would water just looking at it. It'll burn and hurt, and he'll ask me to stop, but I'll laugh. I'll call him pathetic. I'll spit on him and slap his face and drive that dildo into him until he's loose and sloppy enough for me to get my fist inside."

The color drained from Dylan's face. He released Yates's shirt.

"I'm going to shove a cloth in his mouth when he cries for help and keep going, fisting him hard and fast. Brutally. Until he's crying, until snot is running from his nose."

Just how Darius loves it.

"Can you handle that?"

Dylan didn't answer, but he didn't need to. His pale complexion was enough, even the sparkle in his eyes had dulled.

"If you can take his place, I'll cancel on him right now. Can you handle what I described, Dylan?"

"No," he whispered.

Dylan collapsed back into his chair with a stricken expression.

"Exactly, now have a good night, and don't burn down my shop."

Yates zipped up his jacket and left.

He stopped on the pavement outside, again inwardly chanting, "Don't look back", but he did. *Of course, he did.*

Dylan hadn't moved. He looked so small, alone in the flower shop. Yates's flower shop. The bright flowers around him made the scene even more tragic like the bouquets celebrated his sadness. Yates had made him look like that. He'd made him *feel* like that.

"So what?" he spat at the street.

He wasn't the first person Yates's bluntness had upset, but a heaviness pinned down his insides when he watched him in the shop. He didn't like it, but he couldn't look away.

Did he know Yates couldn't leave? Did he know he'd played Yates's heartstring like a fiddle?

"Fuck it," he growled.

Darius whined and bitched at him down the phone. Yates hadn't expected anything else. It was late. No doubt Darius had thoroughly prepped himself and cleared his Sunday to bask in the afterglow. It was the first time Yates had cancelled, and Darius had the guts to call him soft.

He glanced through the window at Dylan. *Fuck, Darius had a point.*

When he pushed into the shop, Dylan didn't glance over. He carried on staring at the floor. "Did you forget something?"

Yates marched straight over to him, gripped the back of his head, and pulled him to his stomach. Dylan didn't hug him back at first. His movements were slow, tentative as if he wasn't sure if he wanted to touch the brute in front of him. Yates retreated, but Dylan came with him, hugging him tightly.

"I'll do a demo, but I'm warning you, it will be shit."

"What about Darius?"

"I cancelled."

Dylan peeled his cheek from Yates's chest. Instead of a smile or a breathed-out thank you, Dylan's brow crumpled, and he shook his head.

"I thought you'd be happy."

"But I can't…"

"Can't what?"

"Do what you described." He exhaled a shaky breath. "I don't want you to do those things to me."

Doing them to Darius pleased a feral part of Yates. Darius loved being tortured into coming, but the thought of doing those things to Dylan? His gut squelched, and his heart started pounding. He shook his head. It wasn't a comfortable image.

"I don't want to do those things to you either, and for the record, Darius asks me to do those things."

"But you said if he begs you to stop, you'll carry on."

"It's part of it. If Darius truly wants me to stop, he'll give me a safe word."

"What is it?"

"Red. If he's gagged and tied, he'll knock two fingers against the headboard. It's consensual pain."

"Consensual?"

"One hundred per cent."

"Sorry…I didn't mean to interrupt."

Yates whirled around, rearing up to tell the intruder to get lost, but Dylan released his hold on Yates and ran to greet the woman. Yates read her banner. Bride-to-be.

"This is my sister, Hannah."

They had the same eyes, but where she looked elated, Dylan looked petrified. He raised his eyebrows. *Act nice.*

"The bride-to-be." Yates forced a smile. "Let me get you a glass of champagne."

Chapter Seven

It was worse than Yates had imagined. The group of women who invaded his shop giggled throughout his demo, butchered his flowers, and spilled champagne all over the place. His shoes stuck to his floor as he trudged into the back to get a mop. Dylan followed him, whispering a soft thank you for the millionth time.

His thanks no longer pleased Yates like they had the first few times. The night dug its heels in and refused to end, and the noise level in the shop steadily increased. Laughs hit higher frequencies, and the sexual innuendos flying around pushed Yates to the limit.

Yates tensed at smashing glass. He whirled around to a wide-eyed Dylan blocking the way.

"I'll get it."

"No," Yates growled. Thunder rumbled in his chest. "You'll only cut yourself."

"They're having a good time at least."

Yates couldn't give a fuck.

Hannah hovered over Yates as he brushed the glass into a dustpan. She gripped the table to stay on her feet, and the champagne glass in her hand looked close to slipping.

"I've been in your shop before."

Yates schooled the anger out of his face before looking at her. "Dylan said. My color palette is too bold apparently."

"The wedding colors are lilac and blush pink."

"Sounds disgusting."

Hannah's brow folded, her hand swayed, and she narrowly avoided tipping champagne down Yates's back. He almost bit his tongue in half not to yell at her.

"What did you say?"

Act nice.

"I said it sounds delightful."

The confusion in her face cleared, and she beamed down at him. "Thank you. None of your flowers would've worked."

"What a shame…"

Yates skimmed his gaze past her. He needed someone to interrupt, someone to save her from his foul mouth he tried his best to suppress.

"Your roses, though." Hannah's eyes rolled. "My God, your roses were like nothing I've ever seen. If we hadn't already picked the chair covers and the bridesmaids' dresses, I would've changed the whole wedding to red to compliment them."

Maybe Dylan's sister wasn't so bad.

"Roses are the queens of all flowers." Hannah chucked more champagne from her glass as she gestured to the shop. "The hell with daisies and daffodils and fucking lilies. It's always the rose. The rose is the statement flower. A red rose says I love you."

She sniffled. Yates threw a desperate look across the room at Dylan. He couldn't deal with a sobbing woman. Hannah wiped her eyes and managed to tip the remaining champagne all over the floor. It splashed Yates's shoes as he got to his feet.

"Sorry, I don't mean to be so emotional."

Yates fought the anger from showing on his face. He smiled, and in Hannah's intoxicated state, she didn't notice the manic grin, the minute spasms of a man trying to hold it together.

"This wedding means so much. I'm going to be happy. We're going to be happy. We are. I know we are…"

Hannah didn't sound convinced. One of the hen party peeled herself away from the group and headed over to Yates. She hugged Hannah and spoke in her ear.

"It was a joke, a stupid joke."

Hannah had hit the overly emotional level of drinking. The rest of her friends gathered around her, but Dylan stayed back.

Yates squeezed past the fawning women and tipped the glass out in the bin out the back. He heard the bell ring and went back inside to welcome the stripper.

"All right, bitches, one of you order something hot?"

Yates winced at the screech of excitement. From crying to screaming, and all it took was a man in uniform. Ranger strutted in dressed as a fireman, pouting and spraying an invisible hose.

It had taken surprisingly little cash to get Ranger to strip. He'd sounded enthused by the idea when Yates called him. By the looks of his bronzed skin, he'd even booked himself in for a spray tan.

"Let's get this party started. I'm warning you, ladies, my hose is loaded and ready to pour."

Yates scrunched his nose up. *Well, that sounded disgusting.*

Ranger wagged his finger at him. "DJ, cue the music."

He raised one eyebrow. There was no music.

Dylan got out his phone. "Song?"

"Fireman Sam," Yates muttered.

Dylan laughed and threw him an amused look. They held each other's gaze for far too long. Ranger cleared his throat. "I charge by the minute."

Yates glared. "No, you don't."

"Song?" Dylan asked.

"How about we start with 'it's raining men'?"

A cliché choice, but what Yates hadn't expected was Ranger to have an actual thought-out routine. He watched with a slack mouth and wide eyes as Ranger stripped like a pro. The ping of his braces on his shoulders got a cheer from the women, and they clapped when he made his bronzed pecks dance and jiggle.

Ranger ripped off his pants and flashed his sequin thong, barely holding everything in. He lifted his leg up on a chair and lunged. Yates turned away at the sight of his testicle playing peekaboo. That was too much Ranger for him.

"Anyone want to burn this perfect peach?"

Yates peeked another look at him. Ranger slapped his ass and encouraged Hannah to do the same. In no time everyone was slapping Ranger's arse, leaving it red. The award on the shelf shone in the corner of Yates's eye. A respectable business tarnished by Ranger's raw arse.

"I think this peach is cooked to perfection, wouldn't you say?"

He directed the question at Yates, and he looked at Ranger with enough anger to burn him to ash.

It got worse when Ranger squeezed his butt cheek and demanded the bride-to-be bite it. She did. No longer sobbing, but in hysterics, as she mauled Ranger's rear end.

"He's good."

Yates turned to Dylan. He hadn't realized he'd edged closer. They stood shoulder to shoulder at the back of the shop.

"He's good at annoying me," Yates said.

Dylan's gaze wasn't on Ranger shaking his hips. He missed when Ranger got out the tabasco sauce and challenged the bridal party to lick it off his chest. The alcohol hadn't only numbed their minds, but their tastebuds too. They licked it off him like it was nothing, but Yates suspected drinking a liter of tabasco sauce would come back to haunt them the next morning.

He laughed at the thought but stopped when he felt the heat of Dylan's eyes on the side of his face.

"Thank you."

He sighed, not looking at Dylan. "You've said that already."

Dylan's gaze didn't leave him. "I know, but I really mean—"

Yates's phone buzzed against his leg. He hoisted it from his tight jeans and read the name.

Seth

"I need to take this…"

He left Dylan and whatever he was about to say and hurried into the back office. The premium roses filled the small room, and he struggled to get to his chair.

"What have you got for me?"

"The name of the guy who wrote the note, the names of the other three guys who have been hired with him. Marshall security. I've got their mobile numbers, and that's given me a location."

"Seth, you are brilliant."

"I know. I've sent you a file. It contains the names, and where I think they are."

"You're certain Mr Stevenson's there?"

"That's where they are."

"Thank you."

Seth snorted. "Any time, Yates."

Yates ended the call and scrolled through his contacts, pressing on Jeromy's name. He opened the laptop and found the file from Seth.

"Yates?"

"Jeromy, I've got four names for you."

"What do you need to know?"

"Everything you can find out about them. I'll send you the names now. The faster you get back to me, the better."

"Understood."

Yates ended the call and scrolled deeper into his contacts. Seth's hunch about Mr Stevenson's location wasn't enough. He needed proof.

"Max?"

"I'm here, Yates."

"I'm going to send you a location and a photograph of a man I want you to observe. I need a positive ID on him."

"Got it."

The door clicked shut behind him, and he spun around to see Dylan.

Yates closed the laptop and placed his phone on the side.

Dylan smiled at him. Yates didn't know whether his red cheeks were a blush or whether the roses reflected off him.

"Good news?"

"Yes."

"You look nice when you smile."

He touched his lips and realized Dylan was right. He smiled at the net closing in on Mr Stevenson.

"Looking nice isn't the same as being nice."

Dylan came closer. "You are nice."

Yates smirked. "I'm not."

"You are to me."

He curled forward and rested his hands on Yates's thighs as he leaned in.

Interesting.

Yates didn't move, he waited. Dylan released a shaky breath before closing the gap between their lips.

It was so gentle and sweet Yates would've rolled his eyes if they'd still been open. *When did they shut?*

Dylan's lips trembled against his, his nerves fed through to his hands, and he gripped on to Yates's thighs. It was too cautious, too uncertain, too annoying, but Yates's cock was rock-hard in his jeans despite the overly cautious kiss.

He pressed back, harder, fiercer, and Dylan retreated.

Damn him.

Yates's chest rose and fell faster. Dylan dangled his carrot of a mouth so close but wouldn't let him maul it. He wanted soft and gentle. He needed the romance of it.

How disappointing.

Yates narrowed his eyes at Dylan, but Dylan's were still closed. His brow twitched; his lashes fluttered. When he leaned in again, Yates kept his eyes narrowed for as long as he could, but Dylan's tenderness chipped away at him. It made his heart thump, and his skin itch.

He accepted Dylan's version of kissing for as long as he could before surging forward with the aim to part Dylan's lips with his tongue. To plunder that sweet little mouth. Dylan backed off.

A growl of frustration rumbled in Yates's chest.

Why bother kissing at all?

It wasn't a kiss, but a pathetic touching of lips. No tongue or teeth or groans. It was utterly pointless, but when Dylan tried again, Yates's heart skipped a beat.

When Dylan's hands slipped behind his neck, he didn't protest despite the gut reaction to break all his fingers. He let him toy with the hairs on his nape and rub his thumb down the top of his spine. He let Dylan kiss the burns on his face and grind his erection into his lap.

Lap?

Dylan had slipped onto his lap at some point. Yates twitched his numb fingers. His nerve endings came to life, stroking something rough. Jeans. He had his hands on the back of Dylan's jeans and helped him balance on his lap.

The most irritating of pressures burned his lips.

Kiss me properly, goddamn it!

Why wouldn't Dylan suck them or bite them or part his own for Yates to taste him? The questions piled up, but he didn't voice them. He swallowed them down, but the need for an answer became more frantic.

He opened his eyes but closed them again as the room spun.

What was happening to him?

The boom of his heart jolted his body. He felt it everywhere. The desire to launch at Dylan and bend him over the desk was there. It was so strong Yates put all his willpower into keeping it at bay. That left him open to being tentatively and helplessly teased. It was a rubbish kiss, the worst one he'd ever had, but each time his lips unstuck from Dylan's with a wet slurp, it went straight to his buzzing cock.

"Fuck." He put all his fury into the word.

He sneered, but it quickly died on his face.

"What is it?"

Did he not know how close Yates was to losing it? How badly he wanted to pounce on him and pin him to the desk. Yates forced his eyes open. The room was a carousel. Everything except Dylan spun together, blurring around them. The dizziness came from his blood surging through his veins with each powerful contraction.

Dylan didn't know he was teasing a beast.

Everything about his expression was soft and innocent.

His lips lifted into a meek smile, and his eyelids drooped in his daze.

Clueless and stupid.

With no inkling the beast he tickled with his lips was so close to eating him.

And fuck did Yates want to, fucking needed to, if only to get rid of the weird feeling wrapped around him.

The door swung open and clattered into the wall.

Yates glared at the woman in the doorway. As he watched, she became clearer, less unfocused in his haze. She stole his attention away from Dylan, and he hated her for it.

"Get...f'ck..." Yates took a slow blink. He'd slurred, actually slurred. "Get the fuck out."

His eyes readjusted on the woman, Dylan's sister, Hannah.

"If I'd known you were sleeping with him, I could've got a discount on the flowers."

She laughed. It cut through him, and the whirling and spinning stopped. Yates could hear the noise in the other room again. The cackles, the music, Ranger whooping. He dropped from his high, back into his wound-up body.

Dylan got off from his lap but didn't turn toward the door. Yates didn't give a fuck if Hannah caught sight of his erection. It was her damn brother that had put it there and left him painfully desperate.

Hannah fanned her face with her hand. "Oh my..."

Yates flared his nostrils when he looked down at himself. Desperate and from what? A stupid kiss that hadn't even involved tongues. A peck to his lips and face. Fingers pulling the hair on his neck. How goddamn pathetic. Dylan shoved a bouquet at Yates, and he reluctantly took it to cover himself.

"What do you want?" he growled.

"I didn't mean to interrupt."

Yates was glad she had. He was either going to fuck Dylan over the desk or come in his pants, and both came with a disturbing lack of control.

But the high had felt good.

"Why did you?" Yates snapped.

"Hmm? Oh right, Gayle's been sick over the counter."

Nothing to sober up his sex-starved mind like sick all over the shop.

"Great. That's just great."

****

Yates didn't understand it. He'd been turned on by the simplest of touches. Skin on skin, and lips on lips. Not just turned on, but feverishly so. Driven to the point of insanity by holding on. He wouldn't have fucked Dylan without asking him first, but if he had, it would've come out shrill and needy.

He would've begged. That made him want to smash something and tug his hair out.

Yates did not beg.

"Hey," Ranger said. "What did you think of my performance?"

"Annoyingly okay."

"Only okay?"

"Good. You were good."

"I heard the bride-to-be caught you feeling up her brother in the closet."

"I wasn't feeling him up."

It was the other way around.

Ranger grinned. "He's been in the shop rather a lot."

"He studies here."

"There's a library less than a hundred yards from here."

Yates said nothing.

"Well, if you're not interested, can I have a crack at him?"

"Absolutely not. He's not your type, and you're not his."

Ranger licked his lips as he studied Dylan on the other side of the room. "Opposites attract and all that."

"I mean it. No."

"Why not?"

He stepped in front of Ranger and blocked Dylan from his heated gaze.

"I said so, that's why."

Ranger smiled.

"What about Darius?"

"What about him?"

"Can I have a crack at him?"

"If you want, but he doesn't want a relationship."

Ranger hummed. "I see."

"You see nothing."

"The fireman sees everything, including this helmet." He tapped the one he was holding. "And your helmet."

"What?" Yates looked down at his crotch, and Ranger burst out laughing.

"Too easy."

"Get out of my shop."

"Later, bitches," Ranger called.

There was less of a cheerful goodbye and more of a groan of pain as the group huddled over buckets. Champagne and tabasco, not a good mix.

Yates called the bridal party taxis and waited for each woman to be collected and driven away. He prayed they'd never return to the shop again. Too many spillages and cackles and dead flowers all over the floor.

Hannah and Dylan were last to go.

"Thank you," Dylan whispered. He blushed and averted his gaze. Yates was having a hard time keeping eye contact with him too. He fidgeted, wanting Dylan to hurry up and leave.

"Don't mention it."

"Hannah had a great time."

Great time showering the shop with sticky champagne and letting her friends spew over the counter.

"And so did I," Dylan added.

He waited, but Yates didn't share his sentiment. He wasn't sure he'd enjoyed the moment in the office. Physically, yes. His blood had boiled, his cock ached and tingled, but mentally... He'd lost all sense of space and time. He'd been weak and helpless, hanging on Dylan's every slight touch but not wanting to push too hard, not wanting to push him away.

He'd been soft.

Yates narrowed his eyes at Dylan. He must've known his effect, known what he was doing. The vulnerable façade had tricked Yates into not seducing him and allowed him to be seduced.

"Yates?"

He blinked himself back to reality and pointed at the taxi. Hannah had her face pressed up against the window, watching them with beady eyes.

"I'll see you tomorrow night."

Dylan flinched like the reminder stung.

"Okay, I'll...see you tomorrow."

Yates didn't wait to see him get into the taxi. He shoved open the door and locked it behind him. The taxi rumbled as it took off from the curb.

Yates waited with his head pressed against the door frame, and once it had gone, he pushed off and turned to face his detonated shop.

Not from a petrol bomb, but because of him offering the place up as a sacrifice.

Never again.

CHAPTER EIGHT

Yates waited on the other side of his net curtain, staring at the pavement outside. He was aware his vigil was somewhat creepy, but he'd spent the last twenty minutes watching Dylan out the window.

Dylan paced the pavement outside the house, throwing panicked looks at the door. Yates could've gone out and pulled him inside, but he didn't. He wanted his prey to come to him.

Dylan's lips moved with words Yates couldn't hear. Yates reasoned it was some kind of self-encouragement because the next thing he knew, Dylan was knocking on his front door.

He smiled and welcomed the weak-kneed gazelle into his den. Dylan staggered inside, clutching his waist. Yates dropped his predatory posturing and gave him a visual once-over. His complexion had paled, his eyes darted all over the place. He'd noticed both things from the window, but the way he held his jacket to this waist set off alarm bells.

"Has someone hurt you?"

He took the edge of Dylan's jacket and opened it to see the damage. No damage, only the annihilator tucked under his armpit. *How hygienic.* He passed the vibrator to Yates like a terrible dealer would pass drugs. Blatantly obvious except to Dylan, who spoke in a whisper, "I've got it."

"Jesus." Yates snorted. Waves of heat emitted from Dylan's cheek, and when Yates relieved him of the vibrator, he sighed like the weight of the world had gone from his shoulders. Yates held it up and waved it over Dylan's head at the street.

"Everybody look. It's a vibrator."

The pavement was disappointedly empty. "Don't," Dylan said, pushing Yates inside and slamming the door. "Someone might see."

"Couldn't give a fuck."

"I don't want everyone knowing."

"You took it home with you on the bus."

"Hidden under my shirt."

Yates smirked. "Bet that looked even more suspicious."

"It was in the box." He narrowed his eyes. "Are we doing this or what?"

Dylan crossed his arms and glared daggers at the floor. Yates quirked his eyebrow. This Dylan was feisty.

"Upstairs, the room where you sicked all over the wall."

"I didn't."

"You did; now get going."

Dylan plodded up the stairs with his head bowed. Yates snorted and pursued Dylan with the vibrator at the ready. He switched it on, and Dylan ran away from the buzzing until he trapped himself in the bedroom.

"This is never going to work if you don't relax."

"This is weird, okay?" He gestured to both of them. "I'm not sure what you want from me."

"Feeling like you've got no control, Dylan?"

He nodded. "Exactly that."

"Good."

It was payback.

"Now take your clothes off."

Dylan licked his lips. "What, right here?"

"No, out in the garden… Of course here."

"Right." Dylan froze with his hands on the bottom of his T-shirt. "Turn around."

"What?"

"Turn around."

"Seriously?"

"Yes, I'm serious."

Yates gritted his teeth and turned to the wall. His eyes locked on the sick mark left behind. The slight stain he hadn't yet painted over. The smell had thankfully gone. Yates sighed; he couldn't wait to be close enough to smell Dylan. His strawberry-scented hair.

"You done?"

"I'm done."

Yates's smile dropped off his face. Dylan had dived under the sheet, hiding from Yates's lusting gaze. He glared at the clothes on the floor, then pushed them into a pile with his foot.

"You'll stay over there, right?"

Yates rethought leaping onto the bed and tipped back onto his heels.

"You want me to stay over here?"

"Yeah, and you'll just talk me through what I should do. Teach me the best way to use it, and then…then we're even."

Yates's hope for a physical lesson in anal play dissolved around him.

"If me being over here makes you more comfortable, then I'll stay here."

"Yes."

Oh. Not the night Yates had been withholding jerking off for. Dylan didn't even look in his direction.

Yates let loose a sigh that was pure disappointment.

"Lube." He tossed a bottle onto the bed, and the vibrator still whirling away. Dylan hurried to switch it off. Yates sighed again. The fantasy of Dylan in his bed was a hundred times better than the reality.

"This was the agreement, remember?"

"I remember." Dylan didn't direct the answer to Yates. He stared at the ceiling, stiff as a corpse.

"Lube up the toy."

He did, with shaking fingers. Yates huffed and collapsed his back to the wall. Why had he thought this would be a good idea? He should've stuck with Darius. When he came over, he stripped naked as he rushed up the stairs and scouted out the lube from the drawer before Yates even caught up. The begging began soon after. *Don't fuck me. Don't force me.* Which in Darius's world meant he wanted the complete opposite.

"And if I don't want to continue, I say red?"

Nothing had even happened.

"Dylan, you're in charge of the toy."

He scrunched his eyes shut. "But if I say red, you'll stop."

Stop what?

"Yes."

"Then what happens?"

Yates frowned. "We stop."

"You'll just kick me out."

Darius had never uttered his safe word. He'd never had to deal with him upset and emotionally vulnerable.

"Yates?"

"I'll help you feel better, let you stay if you wanted to, but if you prefer to leave, I wouldn't stop you. I'd just ensure you got home safely."

"Okay." Dylan swallowed. "So…so what do you want me to do with it?"

What did Yates want Dylan to do with a lubed-up anal vibrator? It was pretty damn obvious. He bit his tongue to stop himself from snapping. If Dylan was trying to kill the mood, he was succeeding in his goal, but Yates's cock was hard anyway. He was angry and hard, and he hated the mishmash of the two, especially when it was becoming obvious he wasn't in for a release.

"Stretch yourself open, take your time. There's no rush. Get comfortable with it before you switch it on."

Dylan placed his feet flat on the bed. The sheet tented over his knees, hiding everything from view. No matter how much hatred Yates put in his glare, the sheet didn't combust and reveal the vibrator edging into Dylan. He waited and waited while Dylan fidgeted about until his patience was hanging by a thread.

"You comfortable yet?"

"Yeah, it's in."

Yates narrowed his eyes. "It's in?"

Dylan hummed. "And it feels good."

A jolt went through Yates's cock, but he ignored it and continued to watch Dylan's face. His completely blank face. The skin under one of Yates's eyes spasmed as he watched Dylan with laser intensity.

"Are you ready to turn it on yet?"

"Turn it on?"

"Yes, the button on the side."

The vibrator buzzed to life. Yates shut his eyes. His frown grew fiercer as he listened. Not the sound of a vibrator inside someone, but one clearly on the outside, buzzing against nothing. If Yates touched the bed, he imagined he'd feel the tremors.

"Is it deep inside you, Dylan?"

He licked his lips. "So deep."

"And it feels good."

"Incredible."

Yates folded his arms, still glaring.

"What?" Dylan asked.

"It's strange, that's all."

"What is?"

"Most guys close their eyes when they're pleasuring themselves with a vibrator."

Dylan's eyes snapped shut.

"And their knees start to tremble."

A category 9 earthquake went through Dylan's legs. Yates rolled his eyes and approached the bed. He stretched his hand out towards the tented-up sheet.

"And they moan, a soft moan in the back of the throat."

Dylan wailed gently. Like a dying gazelle, and Yates was going to be the lion to put it out of its misery.

Yates gripped the sheet and yanked it from Dylan's raised knees. He cried out and scurried up the bed, leaving the vibrator buzzing on the sheet.

"Is there a reason you're pretending?"

Dylan didn't answer. He hid his flaccid cock with a pillow.

"Dylan?"

"It doesn't work!"

He kicked the vibrator away, but Yates caught it before it fell from the bed. Dylan's glassy eyes found Yates, and his eyebrows were performing all kinds of gymnastics as he tried to hold it together.

"The vibrator doesn't—"

"Not the vibrator. Me. I don't work."

"What do you mean?"

"It's supposed to feel good, but it doesn't."

"You're not going to come from it vibrating against your thigh."

"Stop mocking me."

"Stop being so…so…" Yates looked away. "You haven't even tried it."

"I have in my room. I've put it in, turned it on, tried to find something, but there's nothing. I don't have a prostate, okay."

Yates bit his lip not to laugh. "Of course, you do."

"Well, it doesn't work."

"You're nervous, that's all."

"Bet you regret cancelling on Darius now."

His mind said yes, his cock was undecided, but his chest? It was doing its odd beating again. *Damn thing.* Tomorrow he would call the doctor.

"You have a prostate."

"What if I don't?"

"You had sex with your ex."

"He wasn't my ex."

Yates grunted. "Did you have sex with him?"

"We did everything, except…" Dylan's expression sank into despair.

"Except sex," Yates finished.

His heart did its odd thump. He needed to ask a doctor about it.

"I wanted to, really wanted to, but he didn't, and it's a good job he didn't. I can't even do that right."

"Shush." Yates pressed his finger to Dylan's lips. "I can't stand it when you get hysterical. Now lie the fuck down."

Dylan widened his eyes. "What?"

"Lie down."

"Why?"

"I'm gonna find this prostate of yours, prove it's there. That's if you want me to."

The longest few seconds of Yates's life went by, then Dylan whispered the softest yes that had ever been spoken by man.

Thank fuck.

Dylan slipped little by little down the bed. Yates huffed, grabbed his ankle, and pulled him. He yelped but didn't struggle away.

"Relax."

Yates laid down on his side and stroked Dylan's thigh. It stiffened. *Jesus Christ.* He was seconds away from telling Dylan to put his clothes back on and calling the whole thing off, but he held on to his anger and frustration. Some voice in his head told him it would be worth it. He brushed his fingers over Dylan's thigh until his muscles began to soften.

"You said you want to try anal sex."

Dylan's leg clenched again. Yates inwardly screamed. This was never going to work. He drowned out the cynical part of his mind.

"Don't worry. I'm not going to fuck you."

Yates's cock throbbed in his pants. An insistent disagreement.

Dylan swallowed. "Yes, I want to try it one day."

"Why?"

"To know what it feels like, to have that connection with someone else."

That sounded far too emotional for Yates, but he wasn't about to scowl at Dylan, not when he'd slipped his fingers up Dylan's thigh without him forcing all his muscles to contract.

"What do you hope it feels like?"

"Good."

Yates snorted softly. "Give me more than that."

Dylan's eyes slid shut; Yates had his fingers on his taint.

"I just…I think it'll feel good having something press inside me, stretch me."

"You like the idea of someone stretching you."

"Yes."

Yates took advantage of the squeak of an admission and rubbed his forefinger around Dylan's well-lubed hole. He'd at least done that before trying to deceive Yates out of their deal.

"Tell me what else you like the idea of."

Dylan let out a shaky breath. "Taking someone inside me, feeling it slipping in, knowing my body has them."

Yates hummed by his ear. "That's hot."

"I want to be full, and pinned, and pushed into over and over."

Dylan squirmed on Yates's finger as he pushed it inside. It didn't take long for him to find what he wanted. The marble of pleasure Dylan denied he had. Yates experimented with different strokes. His thick finger was being hugged by Dylan's body, and he couldn't help wishing it was his cock being squeezed by the warmth.

"Keep talking."

Dylan panted. "I want a guy to get so worked up inside me he comes. He swells and fills me with his seed."

"I guarantee whoever the lucky guy is, he'll blow his load so fast."

"I want to be told I feel amazing."

"You do feel amazing."

Dylan's head tossed against the bed. A Mexican wave went through his eyebrows.

"Yates?" His throat bobbed with a swallow. "What are you doing to me?"

His voice came out soft.

"I'm stroking your prostate. You seem to like the gentle up and down strokes best."

"What?" Dylan exhaled hard. His lips were completely dry. A pastel pink shade, Yates wanted to bite them darker, but he held back.

"How do you know?"

"Your cock oozes all over your stomach when I do it just right."

He demonstrated, but Dylan didn't open his eyes to watch.

"I can't feel it in my cock. I can only feel that other sensation."

"What sensation?"

He shifted against the bed. "The throbbing, building sensation. It's strange."

"It means I'm doing it right."

Yates relished Dylan's whine when he pulled his finger free.

"Hey, why are you stopping?"

He dared to sound annoyed. Yates smiled and sank two fingers inside. Dylan hissed and threw his hips forward.

"You said you wanted to feel stretched."

"It burns."

He continued rubbing Dylan, easing the pain through pleasure.

"It'll fade. I'm going slow with you."

It was taking every ounce of Yates's control.

"Thank you."

His shaky voice broke Yates's composure. He stopped sinking his fingers in and out and stared at Dylan's relaxed face. His brow began to fold, and his nose twitched.

"Yates?"

He resumed sliding his fingers back and forth and pushed the odd moment to the back of his mind.

"I'm going to push the vibrator into you."

"Why?"

"That's why you're here, remember?"

Dylan nodded. "Okay."

It took time to work Dylan open with the toy and slide it to the right spot. Yates rubbed Dylan's prostate with it before switching on the lowest setting.

"Feel okay?"

Dylan shivered. "Feel's…good."

Yates smiled and grabbed Dylan's hand off the bed. He made Dylan take the toy and experiment for himself. It didn't take him long to get the hang of it.

"When you're about to orgasm, hold off, clench for as long as you can. Trust me, it'll blow your mind when you come."

Dylan didn't reply. Yates doubted he'd even heard him in his blissed-out state. He smirked when he pulled up Dylan's eyelid and saw his eyes had rolled to the back of his head.

"You are so hot, and you don't even know it."

Dylan grunted, and Yates's eyebrows swung up in surprise when the vibrator got louder. He liked it harder and faster according to the moans and whimpers bursting out of him.

Interesting.

Yates pulled down the top of his sweatpants and grabbed his cock. He stroked as he watched Dylan get himself higher and higher.

"It's gonna be fucking embarrassing if I come before you."

He looked at Dylan's drooling cock. The blush pink head, the silky-smooth shaft. The smears all over his torso. What did he taste like?

Yates gripped his cock at the base, wagging it slightly as he got himself under control.

"I can't believe no one has fucked you, or stretched you, or filled you, or hit you at just the right angle that you come all over yourself."

Dylan moaned and pressed the toy into himself with more urgency.

"You have no idea how badly I want it to be me."

The words had left him before he could stop them. Heat grew in Yates's face. *Why had he said that?* He stared at his cock, big and hard in his hand. That inside Dylan. His own eyes felt pulled towards the back of his head. The mental imagery was good, too good.

Dylan turned the toy up another setting and lifted his hips off the bed. "You want to fuck me?"

Yates didn't answer. He brushed his thumb over the side of his cock and imagined the pressure was Dylan's prostate.

"'m gonna come," Dylan murmured.

Thank the fucking Lord.

"Oh fuck, I'm going to come!"

Yates stopped touching himself and stroked Dylan's thigh. "Relax, and let go."

Dylan did, and it was the most beautiful thing Yates had ever seen. His moans came out choked, and his words garbled. He threw his head back, stretching out his throat, his chest, arching off the bed as his cock released wave after wave of come. It didn't come out with speed, but slow surges of cum that lasted longer each time.

It glistened on his chest, and Yates couldn't resist moving over Dylan and ducking down to taste him. He ran his open mouth over Dylan's dirtied chest, covering his lips in cum as Dylan continued to spurt against Yates's chin.

Once Dylan was done, and the toy had fallen silent, Yates licked his chest while jerking his cock hard and fast. He closed his eyes and explored with his mouth and nose.

The small mound of hair at the root of Dylan's cock smelled of strawberries too. He must've shampooed it. Yates nestled his nose into him and got drunk on the fumes of strawberries and come. A winning combination. Strawberries and cream. He licked Dylan clean, humming in deep satisfaction, until Dylan shifted and moaned.

Yates slurped Dylan's re-hardening cock into his mouth and deep-throated him until he was high with the need to come.

Dylan gripped Yates's hair with both hands and called his name. Being slow and gentle wasn't an option; he needed Dylan to orgasm hard and fast into his mouth.

The first hit of Dylan's cum to the back of his throat set off his own orgasm.

He beat himself off and swallowed Dylan down at the same time. Cum shot out of him and splattered Dylan's thighs. Yates released himself and panted for breath, face to face with Dylan's newly dirtied legs. Strawberries and cream. He snorted and threw a glance up to Dylan.

"Sorry. I should've asked."

Dylan licked his lips, panting hard. "I didn't say red."

"No, I guess you didn't." Yates sat back on his heels.

"That was..." Dylan laughed softly. "There's no word for that. Thank you."

"You don't need to thank me."

"Yes, I do."

Dylan gazed at him in a way he didn't like, but he didn't have the heart to growl at him to stop. Instead, he avoided looking back and leaned away from him.

"I'll get us a cloth, clean you up."

"And then what?"

"I don't know about you, but I need a nap."

"A nap with you sounds perfect."

Yates had planned to nap alone in the spare room, but one glance at Dylan and he couldn't crush his happiness. Not when he was smiling softly and shifting over in the bed already awaiting Yates's return.

Lying next to Dylan while they slept, how bad could it be?

CHAPTER NINE

"So you gonna tell me what's up?"

Yates blinked and refocused on Ranger perched on one of the display tables. His shades were hooked over the top of his vest, and he watched Yates with a crocked smile, amusement dancing in his eyes.

"Fine, I'll guess…hemorrhoids?"

"What?"

"But the problem wouldn't be if they were up, but down, as in hanging out."

"Why are you like this?" Yates asked.

Ranger shrugged. "To get your attention. Now tell me what's up?"

Yates huffed. "Nothing's up."

"Oh really?"

Yates curled his fingers into fists. "Really."

"I just sat here and destroyed three roses, and you didn't even notice."

The evidence littered the floor. Premium petals.

"What the fuck, Ranger?"

He shrugged. "I could say the same to you." He squinted. "Except the last part. I wouldn't say my own name to you—"

"Why are you here again?"

Ranger dropped to his feet. "This is what I'm talking about. You messaged me yesterday and asked me to meet you."

Oh.

Yates squeezed the bridge of his nose. "About Mr Stevenson."

"You sick?"

"I'm not sick." Yates looked up. "Then again, maybe I am."

His pulse was irregular, he had pains in his chest, and whenever he flicked his gaze over to Dylan's desk, it worsened. Not Dylan's desk. It was a goddamn flower table, an empty one. Yates pushed off from the counter and trudged across the shop. He grabbed the nearest lot of plants and dumped them on the empty table. Less of an eyesore, but still a sore, right in Yates's chest.

Three days since Dylan had trapped him into sleeping in the same bed with his puppy dog eyes. Three days since Dylan had sprawled over him and dribbled on his chest. Three days since Yates had found out having Dylan in his arms wasn't so bad.

It had been verging on nice. Nice? Yates didn't do nice. He growled and snapped the stem of a lily. He had an intense urge to break another with his teeth.

"You're scaring me, and I don't think it's intentional, which makes it ten times more terrifying."

"I'm fine." Yates huffed. "Focus," he said to himself. "I messaged to tell you about Mr Stevenson."

"You know where he is?"

Yates nodded.

"Then why are we out here? Show me."

Ranger led the way to the office but was sensible enough not to sit down on Yates's seat.

"We've got a location," Yates said as he woke the laptop. "He's hiding out in some mansion in St Ives. Coastal views. Acres of land."

"Sounds nice."

Yates showed Ranger an aerial view of the property.

"Right on the edge of a cliff."

Yates hummed. "Not ideal for us."

He swapped to his files and opened a folder courtesy of Max.

"Jesus," Ranger muttered. "I think old age might get him first."

The photographs had been taken from a long lens. The sea, visible in the distance. There wasn't much variety to the shots. Mr Stevenson hobbled around the house with his cane. Dark sunglasses covered his eyes, and his wiry hair looked thinner than in the other photographs Yates had of him.

"Killing him will be easy. It's the two security teams we've got to worry about."

"Two?"

Max hadn't only snapped photographs of Mr Stevenson but also of the men protecting him. Not four like Seth had first thought. Jeromy had his work cut out finding usable information about all of them.

Yates nodded. "Different companies, eight guys in total."

Ranger's eyes bore into the side of his face. "This feels like it's a direct challenge. Kill me if you can."

"I think it is, and that's exactly what we're gonna do."

"Eight security guys, one target in a mansion on a cliff... We need help."

"I'm not asking Donnie."

"We need him."

"He and Elliot are supposed to be keeping a low profile."

"Yates—"

He smashed his fist down on the desk. "I'm not asking him, okay? We can handle it."

"He'll want to help."

"Well, Donnie never knew what was best for him, did he? He's got Elliot; he's happy. Why risk his happiness?"

Ranger disappeared from above Yates's shoulder. "But you'll risk mine?"

"That's not what I meant."

"This is sounding like a suicide mission. They know we're coming."

"I'm sorting it," Ranger said. "When have I ever led you into danger?"

The shop door dinged, and Yates slammed down the laptop. Ranger leaned back and checked who'd come in.

"It's the student."

Dylan.

Yates punched his heart for picking up pace. Damn thing.

"Over here," Ranger called. "We were just having a quicky in the office."

"Don't tell him that."

Yates pushed past and went to greet him. They came to a stop two feet from each other and stared. Dylan adjusted his rucksack on his shoulder, still smiling softly. Yates was certain his smile had morphed into something savage, not directed at Dylan, but himself for bounding up to him and not having a clue what to say. *What a fucking idiot.*

Ranger appeared out of the corner of his eye and sprinkled rose petals over Yates's head.

"What the fuck are you doing?"

"Making this moment even more awkward."

Dylan pointed at the plant on his desk. *Not his goddamn desk.*

"Is there no room for me any—"

"There's room," Yates said, sliding the pot aside.

Dylan sat down on his chair and dumped his rucksack onto the table. Yates backed away with Ranger following on his heel, chuckling down his neck.

"Don't," Yates warned. He stood behind the counter, putting distance between them.

"Wasn't going to say anything."

"Good."

"But now that you brought it up, what the hell is going on with you?"

Yates read the warning behind the counter.

DON'T ATTACK THE CUSTOMERS.

"Huh… Ranger, have you ever actually bought anything in here?"

"Why buy it when I can take it for free?"

Yates ground his teeth into dust. "So technically, you're not a customer…"

Ranger grabbed the nearest bunch of flowers. "I'd like these, please."

"That'll be two hundred pounds."

"The label says thirty."

"It's two hundred for you."

Ranger lifted his chin and grinned. Yates toed closer and closer to crossing the line and ignoring Donnie's advice.

"That's a case for trading standards. It's illegal to change the marked price at the tills. You can be fined thousands for that offence. Would probably put you out of business."

"Motherfucker."

Dylan slapped his hand over his mouth, but Yates still caught the sound of his laugh.

"You. Eyes down, study," Yates said.

Dylan licked his lips. "Yes, sir."

"Sir?" Ranger whispered. "The plot thickens. Now, are you gonna tell me what's going on with you two?"

Yates didn't know himself. He'd spent three days trying to wrap his head around it. His conclusion: all the men that had submitted, and begged, and pleaded to him had already been broken in, ready to be taken charge of, but Dylan hadn't. It made him vulnerable and satisfying in a way the others hadn't been. It had never appealed to him before, and he'd never thought he'd have the patience, but Yates had enjoyed exposing him to anal pleasure.

He wanted to do it again.

"What you reading?" Ranger asked.

Dylan glanced up from his book. "Treasure Island."

"Ah, good old Captain Hook. Has Yates shown you his hook? Bit different to a pirate one. Goes in your asshole."

Dylan dropped his book on the table. His mouth opened wide enough to catch birds, let alone flies.

"There's no Captain Hook in 'Treasure Island'," Yates muttered.

"Course there is. He's the one who fights the dragon."

Yates banged the heels of his hands onto his forehead. "Are you like this on purpose?"

"Like what?"

The doorbell rang, and Yates glanced over, only to freeze and widen his eyes. Adam's gaze tracked the floor as he made his way to the counter.

"Edna, is she…?"

"The infection took its toll. She's in a coma, the doctor he…he's saying we should prepare for the worst."

The overly optimistic doctor was saying that? Edna was as good as gone.

"Thanks for telling me."

Adam nodded but didn't back away from the counter.

"Is there something else?"

"No. Yes. Kinda. Do you have a leaflet or something?"

"A leaflet?"

"You know, for flowers and wreaths and things like that."

DON'T ATTACK THE CUSTOMERS.

Adam had never bought anything. Yates sidestepped out from behind the counter and bulldozed into him. He tightened his hands into Adam's jacket and shook him while backing him up across the shop. The windows shook as Yates pinned him against the door. He moved his hands to Adam's neck and basked in the terror emitting from his eyes.

"She's not dead yet, but you…you are."

"Yates!" Dylan burrowed in the gap between him and Adam, pushing against Yates's chest. He released Adam's neck and took a step back as he choked and gasped, sprinkling spit all over the doormat. Yates pushed out his chest, ready to go at him again, but Dylan stood in the way, putting all of his strength into holding Yates at bay.

"You're a lunatic." Adam flung open the door and fled down the street.

"Why did you stop him?" Ranger asked. He eyed the ceiling, deep in thought. "Wait… How did you stop him?"

"What do you mean how? I got between them and pushed Yates away."

"Trust me, you never pushed Yates away, he backed up. Hey, why did you back up?"

Yates didn't answer. He stood heaving for breath, fighting against every instinct to launch from the shop and chase Adam down the street.

"I had to stop you," Dylan whispered. "You couldn't kill him."

"No. Think of the reviews." Ranger hummed. "Actually, not a bad advertisement. Bloomers: so serious about funeral wreaths, they'll kill over them."

Dylan drifted over to his desk and started to pack his rucksack.

"What are you doing?" Yates asked.

"You're gonna visit your friend, right?"

Ranger barked a laugh. "Come off it. I'm his best mate, and he didn't visit me when I was in a coma."

Yates's stomach twisted.

"He didn't visit you?" Dylan asked.

"Nope. Donnie did, our other best mate, but not Yates."

"There was no point. It doesn't help; it doesn't do anything. It's a waste of time."

Dylan flinched. "She might appreciate you being there."

"She won't know."

"But—"

"There's nothing I can do for her, so leave it, both of you, just leave it."

Ranger held up his hands. "I'm off."

"Good, get out."

Yates pushed past him and trudged into the office. The bell rang, signaling Ranger and Dylan leaving. Yates sighed, opened up the laptop, and searched for a place to find a quick and convenient lay. He was no good with emotions and sentiment, but sex… That was easy, that was simple.

"What are you doing?"

Yates gritted his teeth at Dylan's question and carried on scrolling the website, searching.

"You should've left."

"I wanted to see if you were all right."

He paused, then shook his head. "I'm fine."

"Are they escorts?"

"This is none of your business." He clicked on one at random, hoping to get the message across, but Dylan didn't leave.

"Why?"

"I need a distraction," Yates said.

"Is this what you do whenever you get bad news?"

"Go home, Dylan."

"Take me home…with you."

Yates breathed out a slow breath.

"I can be a distraction."

"I'm not doubting it for a second, but I'm not sure you're the right distraction."

"What does that mean?"

"You mess with my head."

"What?"

Yates shook his head and shifted to get his wallet from his jeans. Dylan snatched it from his hand.

"I want to go home with you."

Yates twisted around to face him. "And I want to play around with a guy who knows what he's doing."

Dylan shrunk in on himself and dropped the wallet into Yates's palm. He didn't move away; he seemed intent on watching Yates type in all his details and make the booking. He got to his card number, then slammed the laptop lid down and gripped his head.

"Fine," Yates said. "I'll take you home with me."

****

Yates opened up the closet of sex toys, and Dylan stepped inside with panic-blown eyes. He pointed at each toy, and Yates replied what it did in a deadpan voice. Dylan backed away from some as if they might leap off the shelves and attack him. Yates slumped when he disregarded the cuffs and restraints. He wanted nothing more than to tie Dylan up and stuff a butt plug in him. A small one. Some of the ones in the closet were monsters. Some vibrated, some even gave off electric shocks. Dylan ignored them all.

"Anything?"

"I'm still looking."

He pointed a shaking finger at a clear masturbator on the wall. "Does that go in or out?"

Yates rolled his thumb against his temple and sighed. "You go in it."

"It's over ten inches long. Who has a cock that big?"

"A few guys are gifted, but that toy isn't for one; it's for two. Both cocks go in at opposite ends. It's ribbed inside, and it vibrates too. You can take turns stroking."

"It's still in its packaging."

"Yeah, well…"

Yates didn't explain why; he didn't have to explain himself. Dylan had hijacked his night of fun—again. Yates owed him nothing. Dylan's fingers stopped trembling when he touched the box. He traced the letters. The Head Kisser.

Anything but that.

Yates steered Dylan's attention to the far wall and the anal beads. "These will be good for you just starting out, the smaller beads. I lube them up, slip them in, then pull them out when you're close to coming. If you like the masturbators, I've got a couple of solo ones. Some sleeves, some fleshlights. We could use them at the same time."

"I want to use the double masturbator."

"Dylan…"

"You said I could pick what I wanted to try, and I want to try this." He grabbed the box off the shelf and gave it to Yates.

"Is it because it's sealed? I've got other sealed toys if you—"

"I like that we'll be face to face."

Which was one of the reasons Yates did not want to use it.

"We'll be able to kiss."

That was the other reason.

Dylan rushed past and jumped on the bed. He bobbed up and down on his knees, eager to get going, with no hint of nerves or fear. One session of anal play and Yates had corrupted him already.

He groaned. "I need to clean it."

"Don't be long."

Yates took some anal beads to clean too and returned to a naked Dylan on the bed. He had the sheet over him, but it wasn't tented by his knees and his erection was visible.

"Did I do something wrong?"

"No." Yates's voice came out strangled. "No, nothing wrong."

He placed the toys on the bed and removed his clothes while Dylan watched. He licked his lips and eyed Yates with hunger, focusing on his cock as it swung free. Yates gave it a few pulls, and Dylan couldn't tear his eyes away.

"How do we do this?" Dylan asked.

"Get on your knees; I'll lube it up."

Dylan did as he was told, but he no longer bobbed with excited energy. "Are you sure I've not upset you?"

Yates snorted. "You couldn't upset me if you tried."

He speared his slippery fingers into one end of the toy before spinning it around and doing the other.

"I'm supposed to be a distraction, but I'm not doing a very good job."

Dylan dropped the sheet from covering his body. Fuck, he had a lovely cock. Yates finished spreading lube into the dual masturbator, then crushed the center cavity with his hand.

"Put your cock in."

Dylan grabbed the end and slipped himself inside. His mouth dropped open as he fucked into it. Yates's cock trickled, but Dylan was too distracted to notice.

"I told you it was ribbed."

Yates pushed his cock inside as far as it would go, then released his grip on the center for an extra bit of suction. Dylan gasped. He bowed, and his hands gripped onto Yates's shoulder. He hadn't even turned it on or started to stroke them, but Dylan was already close to blowing. *How disappointing.*

It would take longer to clean than Dylan would take to ejaculate.

"I'm gonna turn it on."

"Okay," Dylan whispered.

Yates pressed the button, sending vibrations through the masturbator. Dylan gasped and gripped Yates's shoulders harder. He didn't complain about the nails cutting into his flesh, if anything, it was the only hot thing Dylan was doing.

As soon as Yates began pumping their cocks together, Dylan was moaning, begging for a kiss Yates refused to give him. He came after nine tugs, dirtying the masturbator and washing Yates's cock with his come. His cock twitched. That felt kinda nice. Yates looked down at the dirty toy, Dylan's cum was all over the head of his cock. He jerked himself, but Dylan's spent cock flailed around as if he was on fire and killed any hint of arousal.

Dylan slipped himself out. "Too sensitive. I'm sorry."

"Why?"

"I ruined it."

Agreeing with him was on the tip of his tongue, but Yates held it back. Dylan wasn't the one ruining it. It was him. Inviting Dylan over hadn't been a good idea. He wasn't in the mood to be patient and play teacher.

"Maybe you should..."

"Don't tell me to go."

His words sliced Yates through the chest. He didn't voice the rest of them. Dylan's eyebrows flexed, pleading with Yates to let him stay.

He couldn't compete with that.

"We'll try again in a minute."

"Yeah?"

Yates nodded. "Can I put these inside you while we wait?"

He held up the beads. Dylan cowered, but when they didn't bite him, he kneeled up straight again.

"Okay."

Another whisper. Yates lubed them up and pulled Dylan forward on his knees. Their chests pressed together as Yates carefully worked them into his arsehole.

"But if I don't like it…"

"You say red, and I'll remove them as gently as I can."

Dylan slumped against Yates, his heartbeat began to calm, and he sighed contently as Yates inserted the string of beads into him.

"Do they feel okay?"

"Yes, I can barely feel them once they're in."

"The fun comes when I pull them out." Dylan stiffened, and Yates whispered in his ear. "Really slowly. It'll feel amazing, trust me."

Trust me? Where had that come from?

"I do."

His stomach sank at the admission.

Yates averted his gaze and grabbed the masturbator. When he held it up, Dylan's cum dribbled from one of the holes, and his stomach flipped.

"Why haven't you tried it before?" Dylan asked.

Yates pushed his cock into it, making sure to crush the middle for the extra sucking stimulus. "It didn't appeal to me."

Dylan lined himself up and bit his lip as he sank his cock back into it. "Why not?"

He met Dylan's eyes, and a wave of tingles went through his skin. That was the reason. It was too intimate, too romantic. Before he had a chance to sneer, Dylan took the initiative and switched the vibrator on. He jolted and fidgeted before settling down to the rhythm with a breeze of a laugh.

"Hopefully I won't ruin it this time."

Yates took hold of the toy and began to stroke them. "You didn't ruin it the first time."

Dylan leaned forward and began kissing Yates's neck. He refused to retreat but stiffened as Dylan sucked up his throat and tugged his ear with his teeth. Everything about his touch was infuriatingly fleeting, featherlight. Yates hated it, but his eyes fluttered shut, and he breathed evenly as he pumped their cocks.

Dylan pulled back sharply. "I cut you."

"Huh?"

"Your shoulders."

Yates could no longer feel the burn of his pierced shoulders, but when Dylan began soothing the nail marks with his tongue, it reawakened the sensation in his skin. The gentle licks and suction left his heart booming. He dropped his head forward, and Dylan moved to kiss the side of his face, giving him a perfect view of their cocks, head to head. With each stroke, they stretched the middle cavity, slipping and sliding their glands together, aided by lube and Dylan's cum. His cock tingled, and the visual imagery added to the effect.

Dylan kept kissing Yates softly; the sound of his lips and the constant buzzing drove him crazy.

"Fuck," Yates grunted.

He brushed his head against Dylan's to get to his mouth, and then they were kissing. The teasing kissing of the flower shop office. Teasing, and coaxing, and maddening until Yates's brain got all fuzzy. He closed his eyes, and instead of one point of contact, he felt two. Dylan's mouth teasing his, and their cock heads mashing together. It was too much.

Something in him snapped. "Jerk me off."

He stopped stroking, and Dylan took over. It was Yates's turn to use Dylan's shoulders for balance. He fucked the toy with brutal thrusts while thinking of fucking Dylan, pushing deep into him. Hitched breaths escaped Dylan with each piston of Yates's hips. His eyes were awed, his red lips parted. He looked so goddamn perfect taking each harsh blow from Yates.

His cock pulsed, cum erupted, filling the toy. He shoved into the toy riding out his orgasm.

"Yates, I'm so close."

He snapped to his senses and took over stroking. He winced at his oversensitive cock, but kept going, not wanting to break the moment. Dylan held on to him, chanting, 'Oh God,' over and over, and just as he hovered on the cusp of coming, Yates reached behind him and tugged at a bead.

It set him off like a rocket, throwing him forward into a kiss. Yates couldn't resist; he parted Dylan's mouth and licked into the wet heat.

Yates removed the beads as his cum squirted, filling the masturbator. He could no longer see the tips of their cocks, but could feel their warm cum encasing them. It did strange things to Yates's chest, and when he met Dylan's eyes, things got worse. Their connection sparked something, something Yates sure as hell didn't want, but he didn't break away. He ruffled Dylan's hair, then kissed him on his waiting mouth.

Dylan collapsed onto the bed, panting. "That was intense."

Too intense.

Yates hadn't a clue what was happening to him, and he wasn't sure he liked it.

CHAPTER TEN

The next morning, Yates brushed his teeth with more force than necessary. He'd untangled himself from Dylan's hold and retreated to lick his wounds in the bathroom. Yates needed to put a stop to whatever the hell was going on between them. He paused when he heard jingling bells and rolled his eyes.

"What are you doing?" he shouted, glancing at the bathroom door in the mirror.

"Nothing."

"That's a lie. Try again." Yates shoved his toothbrush on the side and stepped out of the bathroom. Just like he'd suspected, Dylan was no longer lounging across the bed but had sneaked into the closet.

He wore only his boxers, and Yates ran his gaze over his pert arse. How was he supposed to stop lusting after Dylan when he had a cute arse like that?

Dylan glanced over his shoulder. "I was just looking."

Yates squeezed his eyes shut to *stop* looking.

"Looks like you were touching to me…"

"Most of your toys look more like torture devices."

"Sexual torture," he hummed, spying the item in Dylan's hand. "Nipple clamps."

"How can that feel nice?" Dylan shuddered. "And why put jingly bells on them."

Yates reached for them and shook the bells by Dylan's ear. "If you use them enough, the sound alone will turn you on and make your cock desperate."

"That must be awkward when it comes to Christmas."

Dylan covered his nipples with his hands. Yates was close enough to smell him, strawberries, like usual, with an added whiff of sweat and cum. Yates's cock throbbed with interest as he sucked in the smell of him.

"They sound painful to me," Dylan said.

"You've got to work up to them...here." He pulled open the closest draw, leaning closer to brush his chin across Dylan's shoulders. "Nipple suckers. That's your starting point."

The tops of Dylan's ears blushed. "They look like thimbles?"

Yates hummed in agreement, abandoning the clamps in favor of the tiny silicone cups. He took Dylan by the wrist and shook him until he opened up his palm.

"You can take them home with you. Use them with the annihilator."

"I wouldn't know what to do," Dylan said.

His voice came out innocent, naïve; Yates knew better now. He knew Dylan teased, acting all clueless.

"Wet the edges, squeeze the cup a little, and stick them on. They'll suck your nipples until they are nice and sensitive."

"Show me."

He spun around to face Yates, still blushing but not avoiding Yates's gaze. His breath hitched as he held his palm out to Yates and twitched his eyebrows. Yates shuffled, his cock ached, but he didn't spare it a glance. He knew it was hard, barely an inch from Dylan's, also hard. He needed Dylan to leave, but Dylan looked like he had other ideas.

"You said I could pick."

"That was yesterday."

"Can't I have more?" Dylan licked his lips. "Don't you want to play with me?"

Motherfucker.

Yates took the suckers from Dylan's hand and kept pressing eye contact while wetting them with his tongue. Dylan's throat bobbed as he swallowed. He stuck his chest out to receive the small cups, shuddering when they made contact and latched on.

"Do they hurt?" Yates asked, twisting them.

His stomach somersaulted at the flinches and spasms in Dylan's face when he turned them.

"A little. More like a warm throb than sharp pain."

"That's what they should feel like."

"Yates?"

"Yes, Dylan?"

"Will you touch me?"

Yates flared his nose, glancing down to Dylan's boxers. The tight material hugged his shape, and for a moment, Yates almost gave in and palmed him through the fabric. Instead, he reached for a single masturbator off the shelf, ignoring Dylan's huff of disappointment.

"I'll touch you with this."

Toys equaled boundaries, and Yates needed them. He pulled Dylan out of the cupboard, spun him around, then pushed him on the bed. Dylan yelped, scrambling up, waiting for Yates to join him.

A generous amount of lube went into the masturbator while Dylan watched with wide eyes. If the night before was anything to go by, Yates knew Dylan was a quick finisher. The sooner he came, the sooner he would leave, and Yates could continue licking wounds he didn't quite know how to heal.

Yates eased off the nipple suckers while Dylan panted as if he was in agony before a soothing lick settled him down again. He pinched the engorged flesh with his teeth, pinning Dylan when he tried to flail and fight.

"If... If I say red, will you stop?"

"Is that you saying red?"

Dylan reared up. "No!"

Yates chuckled. "Good, but the answer is yes. If you say red, I will stop. Always."

Licks and nibbles to his nipples got the loudest response and firm, fast strokes with the masturbator left him fidgeting and fisting the sheets.

Just like Yates predicted, it didn't take Dylan too long to dirty his toy. He pulled it off Dylan and stared at it intently as Dylan panted and wheezed for breath.

He hated his toys getting dirty. It was inevitable. They were designed for it, but still, a dirty toy needed cleaning, and that distracted Yates away from lust, except for when Dylan dirtied his toys.

A toy dirtied by Dylan needed more dirt. Yates tugged down his boxers and thrust his cock into the masturbator, fucking himself with Dylan's cum. His technique was brutal, the same way he'd taken the frustration out on the duel masturbator the day before. He needed it, hard and fast and unforgiving. He pinned Dylan to the bed with one hand, staring at his face while fucking himself in a frenzy until his arm ached.

He came with a gruff shout, filling the toy until cum spilled out, dripping down his balls.

Yates's breathing came in great rasps. He sat back on his heels, watching a dazed Dylan idly toying with his nipples. They stayed as they were, not speaking, just breathing until Yates's heart resumed an inaudible beat in his chest.

"Is that what you'd do to me?" Dylan asked.

Yates opened his eyes, unaware he'd even closed them in the first place. "Yes." He dropped the toy beside them with the nipple suckers and leaned his body over Dylan's. He traced his finger around Dylan's parted lips. "I want to fuck you hard in the mouth...and hard in the arse."

"Okay."

"Okay?"

Dylan nodded. "You can do it."

Yates rolled his eyes and climbed off the bed. "It's time you leave."

"Did I say something wrong?"

"No, but you're a distraction, and I've got things to do."

Dylan snorted. "Like anyone will miss you not opening up Blooming Bloomers for one day."

He found Dylan's T-shirt on the floor and flung it at him. "You're a little shit."

Fuck! Yates froze in horror.

That time, he'd sounded word for word like Donnie. Again.

****

Had he hit a midlife crisis? It was one of many explanations Yates had come up with. His other favorites were he'd gone crazy, and it was all a dream. The latter idea dissolved when a rose thorn went through his thumb.

Damn it.

He dabbed off the blood on his poppy print shirt.

Yates wasn't a relationship kinda guy. He was a fuck and run, except he didn't do the running, the other guy did. Apart from Darius. He got off on bad moods and fear, which Yates was perfect for.

Yates's phone buzzed on the counter, flashing Darius's name. He ignored it and put the phone on silent. His missed calls stacked up, but he didn't want the stress of dealing with Darius's bitching, and he didn't want to arrange to meet because of Dylan.

All the things he'd mocked Ranger for, he started to see the appeal. He'd dragged Dylan into the shower, washed his hair while grinding their cocks together until Dylan spunked down his thigh. Cooked him breakfast, sent him out of the door with a bottle of water and two cereal bars. Even seeing Dylan's left behind jacket had given him a warm fuzzy feeling in his chest.

Darius was right; he'd gone soft.

But that wasn't a bad thing when it felt good, right?

No harm was being done, no crime committed. Yates huffed.

Dylan rushed past the window and threw himself at the door to the shop. It swung open and battered a table. Yates winced, but the glass didn't shatter like he expected.

"What the—"

"I'm sorry."

Yates straightened. "Why, what have you done?"

"My sister's coming over."

Wheels screeched as a car pulled up on the other side of the street.

"I've met your sister before, remember?"

She'd tipped champagne all over the shop, then started blubbering. Yates wouldn't be able to forget her in a hurry.

"I know, but she's gonna ask you."

"Ask me what?"

Yates spotted her climbing out of the car. She linked arms with a guy, then started crossing the road. She waved and called out to Dylan, who stood frozen inside the shop.

"What is she going to ask me?" Yates asked.

"If you'll come to the wedding."

That wasn't going to happen.

"Don't worry; I'm busy that day."

Dylan nipped his bottom lip. "But you don't know what day it is."

"Hey," Hannah said over Dylan's shoulder. She shoved him in the back, and he stumbled into Yates's chest. He caught Dylan, but he pushed away as if burned and knocked his hip into another table.

"You done trying to break the shop?"

"Sorry," Dylan murmured.

Yates turned his attention to Hannah and the painfully plain guy attached to her. Plain white shirt, plain blue jeans, plain brown hair. Utterly boring.

"Have you recovered after the Tabasco sauce?" Yates asked.

The guy glued to Hannah's side frowned at her. "Tabasco sauce?"

"What happens on a hen do, stays on a hen do. Right?"

Yates didn't answer, but Dylan laughed awkwardly.

"This is my fiancé, Rick."

Rick lifted his chin in Yates's direction with a barely audible "All right?"

Yates inclined his head back. "Not bad, you?"

"I'm all right too."

Hannah untangled her arm from Rick's and clapped her hands together. "Look, they're getting on so well already."

Oh please.

"Is there something I can help you with, Hannah?"

She grinned at Dylan coyly. "There is, actually. As you know, we're getting married."

The dopey look she gave Rick made Yates's stomach roll. She held her hand up, flashing her diamond engagement ring.

Yates stared at it. "Yes, that's a ring…"

"And I know you and Dylan have only just started dating."

Dating?

He stared at Dylan, who looked as if he wanted to sink into the floor. His cheeks glowed red, and he didn't look over despite everyone watching him.

"And I was wondering if you'd…."

Yates had his decline ready to go. He'd even forced his brow to fold with regret, but Hannah didn't finish. She looked past Yates to the flowers, and her smile faded.

"They're yellow."

Edna's favorite.

"So what?"

Hannah's face soured, and she spun around to Rick. "Is this where you bought them?"

He groaned. "Not this again. I told you, it was only a joke."

"Not a very funny one. We're getting married in two weeks."

Yates squeezed the top of his nose. "What joke?"

"He gave me flowers with a message that said 'to my bit on the side.' Can you believe that?"

"It was months ago."

She pushed Rick's shoulder. "Did you get them here?"

"No, I got them somewhere else."

Rick turned to her. He craned his head forward, stretching out his neck. His tattoo peeked above his collar. Barbed wire. Yates darted looks between Rick and Dylan.

What the hell was happening?

Rick smoothed a strand of hair behind Hannah's ear and assured her the flowers had been a joke. The flowers. Yates's flowers. Rick must've picked them off the bench outside the hospital, and why had he been at the hospital? Yates flicked his gaze to Dylan. Dylan, who'd been standing on the hospital rooftop, watching as Rick left.

Like a horrible dream sequence, bits and pieces slid together. Rick had been grinding into Dylan and slobbering all over his neck in the alley. Rick was the ex that wasn't an ex. He'd never been a boyfriend in the first place. Yates's brain ached. Hannah's fiancé. He was the reason Dylan had spiraled and couldn't turn to anyone.

Piece of shit.

"Ask me."

Yates destroyed the loved-up display in front of him with a growl and gestured for Hannah to speak.

"Oh, right, yes. I was wondering if you'd like to come to the wedding?"

"I'd love to."

For the first time since Rick had stepped into the shop, Dylan dragged his gaze off the floor. He raised a questioning eyebrow, but Yates ignored it and sidled up to him.

"If that's okay with you?"

Dylan crumpled his brow. "Yeah, sure."

"You don't sound very enthusiastic."

"I am," Dylan said with a half-laugh, but his eyes betrayed him. They flicked to Rick, who didn't react, well-trained in the art of deception. Yates envisioned pummeling him into the floor, but something more dire picked at his gut. Something else left his insides uncomfortably hot with acid. Dylan loved Rick, or he had when he and Yates had first met.

Did he still?

He wanted to know. He *needed* to know.

Yates wrapped his arm around Dylan's waist and pulled him closer. For a few seconds, Dylan went with him, pressing into Yates's side; all was right in the world. The feral part of Yates that had wanted to throttle Rick there and then settled with a purr.

Then it all went to hell.

Dylan stiffened and struggled free. Another guilty glance at Rick. He took a step away from Yates and held his hand up for him to keep his distance. The feral part of Yates growled and ripped its claws into Yates's insides. It wanted to be let loose, but Yates forbade it.

"Come on, they don't wanna see that."

Dylan kept his voice light and teasing. He even threw in a bonus chuckle. *Well played.* The rejection slapped Yates square in the face, but he'd be damned if he let Rick see it.

"We'll save it for when we're alone."

Hannah pressed her hands on either side of her face and beamed. "I'm so happy you're happy."

"It's early days," Dylan said.

His words stung more than Yates imagined they would, but he smiled along, clenching his fists behind his back.

"It's on the twenty-ninth of June, in St Austell. I'll get Dylan to give you all the details."

"I'm looking forward to it."

"Me too," Hannah squealed. "It's a dream come true, five years and he'll finally put a ring on it."

"Five years?"

"I know; talk about taking your time. Now, I'll leave you two alone so you can smooch some more in the office."

"What's that?" Rick asked.

Mr Ordinary continued to look ordinary. Unaffected. He played the game so well.

"On the hen do, I walked in on them making out."

Dylan scratched the back of his neck. "I'd had a lot to drink."

He sank the blade into Yates's chest a little bit deeper. Explaining away *that* kiss. In that moment Yates hated Dylan as much as Rick.

Before Yates could stop her, Hannah leaned in and kissed him on the cheek. "See you soon."

She waited by the door for Rick, who stuck his hand out to Yates.

"Nice meeting you."

Yates didn't shake his hand. He knew he'd end up breaking every bone in his hand if he attempted that. In fact, he'd do more than that; he'd smash his head into Rick's jaw and tear the awful tattoo from his neck with his teeth.

"I better not." He looked at Dylan and stretched near to Rick. "We got carried away in the office before you got here; he made such a mess."

Rick recoiled and snatched his hand back. His plain face cracked, and he threw a disgusted look at Dylan but quickly turned it into a warm smile and added a cherry on top in the form of a chuckle. "That's too much information."

"He's lying," Dylan wheezed. "We never, I just got here."

The blade cut into the cavity of Yates's heart.

"Bye then," Rick said. "Bye, *Dylan*."

"See ya."

Rick opened the door for Hannah. They slipped through and waved as they wandered over to the car.

Dylan exhaled a long breath and slipped his rucksack off his shoulder. "I'm sorry about that."

Yates locked the door and watched Hannah and Rick drive away. There was probably a way to go about this. A gentler approach, spoken with a caring voice while they sat sipping tea. Dylan would break down slowly, revealing all. There would be tears. Maybe they'd hug at the end of it. *Fuck that.* Yates preferred the direct and brutal delivery every time.

"So how long have you been sucking off your sister's fiancé?"

Dylan's mouth opened with a pop. Yates searched his face, the flicker of emotions gearing towards an angry denial. He held up his hand, and Dylan's mouth snapped shut.

"Don't even think about it."

All of his menace went into his words, and Dylan flinched.

"It...I..."

"Your sister's fiancé. How low can you get?"

"It wasn't supposed to—" His voice broke, tears flooded his eyes, and he attached them to Yates. Did he want to be told it would be all right? That these things happened?

Yates curled back his top lip, powered by anger and humiliation. "You're pathetic."

Blubbering, shaking, Dylan's words left his mouth garbled and indecipherable.

"I'm sorry—I didn't...I don't know..."

So goddamn pathetic, but what did that make Yates? Worse than pathetic.

"Your sister."

Dylan dropped his head into his hands, not holding back on the waterworks. They came with sound effects too, great rasps for breath. The sounds ripped Yates's patience to shreds. He'd done what he'd wanted to and got revenge for being humiliated in front of Mr Ordinary. Downplayed and cast off. Yates had been clear it was just sex, but Dylan had insisted on kissing him softly and choosing intimacy with the damn masturbator and asking so sweetly for seconds in the morning. He'd insisted on pulling Yates's arm over him when they were in bed, and when he fell asleep, he'd mounted Yates's chest and stayed there. He'd been sweet and shy and played Yates's emotions with the ease of a fiddler.

He was done.

"Get out."

Dylan dropped to his knees and curled in on himself. He gasped for breath, shaking all over, sobbing through his fingers. Yates's gut twisted into an ugly knot. He thrust open the door and curled his fingers into the wood as he held it.

"I need you to get out."

Dylan didn't unfurl himself from the floor. His breathing came fast and choked. When he moved his hands away from his mouth, he retched.

"You've been sick in my house, don't even think about being sick in my shop."

Dylan retched again. He struggled to breathe, and when he braced his hands on the floor, he let loose his tears and snot and dribble. This level of tragic wasn't a turn-on; it was the opposite. Yates struggled to look at him. His sounds of despair and anguish drove up Yates's anxiety. He wanted Dylan gone so he wouldn't see or hear or feel Dylan's upset in his chest.

"Christ..." Yates hissed. "Stop it. Leave, will you!"

Dylan didn't appear to hear him. The open wounds in Yates's chest bled, each sharp knife Dylan had pushed into him, but somehow he'd avoided cutting his singular heartstring. It danced and quivered with each desperate sob from Dylan.

Motherfucker.

Yates cursed at the outside world, then threw the door shut. The glass shattered, covering the floor. His shoes crunched as he made his way over to Dylan, and he crouched in front of him.

"Come here."

Yates reached for him, but Dylan slapped his hand away. "Don't."

Yates ground his teeth together and persisted, repeatedly reaching for Dylan and getting slapped away. It took ten attempts before Dylan let Yates touch him. Once Yates's hand closed on his shuddering shoulder, Dylan threw himself forward and collapsed into Yates's arms. Still dribbling, and crying, and snotting. Yates got to his feet, bringing Dylan with him. He ruffled his hair, then rested his chin on top of his head as he hugged him tightly.

"It wasn't... It wasn't...supposed to happen."

"Shush." Yates walked him away from the shop entrance and the broken glass. "You need to calm down."

"It... I..."

"Be quiet, or I'll throw you into traffic."

Dylan slumped into Yates's chest, still shaking and sniffling but no longer attempting to justify himself. Yates wasn't sure he wanted to hear Dylan explain. He loved Mr Ordinary, Mr Deceptive Cheating Bastard.

"I'm gonna sit you in the office while I clean up the mess."

Dylan nodded against him, and Yates half carried him into the office before sitting him down at the desk. He grabbed a box of tissues from the top drawer and shoved them into Dylan's chest.

"Clean yourself up."

Yates swept the shop and turned the sign hanging on the doorway to closed. The window repair would have to wait. He headed back into the office where Dylan had stopped crying and retching and instead hiccupped.

"Do you hate me?"

Yates leaned against the wall and crossed his arms. "I don't hate you."

"You should. I deserve to be hated."

"I don't do well with self-pity. Say what you've got to say."

"What?"

"Talk, Dylan, that's what you need. You need to talk. Tell me about him."

Dylan wiped his puffy cheeks. "My first year at uni, I couldn't get into halls. I was so disappointed. I knew I'd have to wait another year. Rick worked nearby; he said he'd drive me there and back. Forty-minute drive. We started talking. I started to like him more than I should. One night he picked me up after a night out, and I kissed him. He pushed me away, and I apologized. But then we started kissing in the car...fooling around."

"Sucking him off, you mean?"

Dylan looked away. "Second year, I got into halls. He didn't need to drive me anymore, and he wanted to cool it off, but I didn't. We argued, we stopped. Every time I thought I was starting to get over him, he'd message, or touch my hand when Hannah wasn't looking, or give me this look. We've only met up a few times in the last few months, but Rick was adamant once he marries my sister, he'll stop it all for good."

"You're gonna let her marry him?"

"What else can I do?"

Yates glared at Dylan. It was obvious, wasn't it?

"Tell her."

"They're good together."

"No, they're not. He's messing around with her brother."

"It's me that pursued him. For four years, they were happy, and then I...I can't undo that."

"He's undone it."

"I complicate things for Rick. It's me that's the problem. Once they're married, Rick's gonna suggest moving north, away from me. I won't see them as much. I'll be able to move on, and they can carry on as if this never happened."

"Your sister deserves the truth."

"Why tell her now? Me and Rick are over. It would only hurt her, and she'll never forgive me if she found out."

"You tell her and you'll lose her; you don't tell her, she'll move away, and you'll still lose her. At least one is honest."

"I couldn't stand it if she hated me." Dylan looked at Yates. "Don't tell her, please."

"This is your family's business, not mine." Yates lowered his gaze. "Do you still love him?"

"I don't know. It's complicated. He's the first guy I've ever had feelings for. You never get over your first love completely, right? That's what people say."

"I wouldn't know."

"Come on, Yates, you must've loved someone?"

He thought about it. The severed strings in his chest curled, then he nodded.

Dylan licked his lips. "Who?"

"My mother, and maybe you're right, Dylan, maybe you never get over it. All you can do is try to forget and make sure you do everything in your power to never feel that way again."

CHAPTER ELEVEN

Yates pulled all his gathered information on Mr Stevenson and came up with a plan of attack. He ran through it with Ranger several times. When it was happening, what weapons they were taking, how they'd take down the security team, and how they'd get away once they were done. A detailed plan, and as always Ranger had been distracted by the pretty flowers in the shop.

"Any problems?"

Ranger stopped petting the middle of a sunflower. "One."

"Okay." Yates took a long breath. "Let's hear it."

"I guess my problem isn't a problem. It's more of a question."

"Get on with it."

"So my question is: Why are you going with Dylan to his sister's wedding?"

Yates looked away. "It's a good alibi."

Ranger quirked his eyebrow. "An alibi?"

"Yes, I'll be seen at the wedding, and the hotel is close by."

"Close by? It's seventy miles away."

"As soon as Dylan falls asleep, I'll meet you, and we'll drive to St Ives."

"And what about my alibi?"

"What?"

Ranger smirked. "You seem to think it's important to have an alibi, and go to the trouble of attending the wedding, staying the night before in a hotel with Dylan and meeting his family for dinner, then the morning ceremony, the wedding breakfast, the buffet in the evening... I'm surprised you haven't been certified to perform the marriage yourself."

"Enough—"

"So I was wondering, where's my well thought-out, overly complicated alibi for the night we butcher a load of people?"

"You don't need one."

"I see."

"Quit it, Ranger."

He slapped his hand to his chest in mock shock. "What am I doing?"

"Fishing for an explanation, and I ain't giving you one."

"I don't need an explanation of why you're going as Dylan's plus one. It's perfectly clear to me, but don't get too swept up in fucking him on the wedding night. Can't have you falling asleep on the job and messing up the hit."

"There won't be any fucking," Yates growled.

He sure as hell meant it. Attending the wedding was the last favor Dylan would get from him. He'd sit next to him, tolerate being his shoulder to cry on, and watch as Dylan's heart crushed in his chest for the final time. Yates was looking forward to the prospect of watching Dylan crumble. He deserved it.

Yates was done being played.

Ranger tilted his head as he studied Yates.

"What?"

"What the hell is going on with you and Dylan?"

"Nothing."

Ranger glanced at the tables in the shop. Yates had cleared one for Dylan as usual, but it was further away from the counter, a yard from the newly repaired door. Dylan's face had dropped when he first saw the new distance, but he'd accepted it and sat down to study.

If he didn't like it, the library was only up the road.

"He seems like he's really into you."

"He's a drama student. A good actor."

"And it seems like you're into him too."

Yates laughed, a bitter laugh that churned up bile in his throat. "Ranger, I'm not like you. I'm not looking for love."

"You're right," he whispered. "You're not *looking* for it, but you found it anyway. I kinda hate you for it."

Ranger smiled, but it didn't reach his eyes.

"Don't mess it up."

"There's nothing to mess up. We have an arrangement, that's all. I will be his plus one at the wedding, and he provides me with an alibi if all goes wrong."

Ranger backed away with his hands raised. "Whatever you say. Tomorrow night, that doesn't give me much time."

"Time for what?"

"Finding my own alibi."

Ranger flung open the door and left.

Yates had performed his good deed. He'd listened to Dylan as he unloaded his thoughts and feelings. Over an hour, Dylan went back and forth from hating Rick to hating himself. Yates listened as silently as he could, and Dylan left with a small smile and the softest of thank yous. Finally unburdened.

The solution Dylan had come to was to let Hannah marry Mr Conniving Ordinary and let them get on with their life. He even dropped in how Hannah and Rick wanted kids, and he was looking forward to being an uncle. It was beyond fucked up, but Yates let it slide.

Dylan's fantasy of everything being all right in the end made him happy. Who was Yates to destroy it? Dylan wasn't his problem despite the pinch in his chest when he whispered a thank you after their talk.

Dylan had lifted up on his tiptoes with his eyes fixed on Yates's mouth. He'd tipped his chin up for a kiss.

Yates had shaken his head in a firm no.

That wasn't happening again.

Dylan's forehead creased as he dropped back to his feet.

Yates's rejection didn't deter him from coming to the shop. He suspected Dylan was afraid he'd back out on being his plus one if he didn't.

One last favor, and then he was done with Dylan for good.

He looked over to the space ready for him to study and swallowed down the jagged lump in his throat.

****

Yates despised people. The sound of them. The smell of them. The sight of them. But most of all, their reaction to him. Before the scars, it had been the tattoos, and before that, his unmovable sneer. The burns on his face drew glances, and stares, and sometimes full-on gawps.

Dylan and Hannah's friends and family were no exception. As the evening dinner went on and the drink flowed freely, the obnoxious people around the table got bolder. They toed the line of asking him what happened but didn't cross over.

"So how did...you find your starter?"

"When did...you buy the flower shop?"

"Why...just...why?"

Dylan's Aunt Margret peered at him through her spectacles, not once meeting his eyes, but she was fascinated by the burn that messed up his eyebrow. She stroked her brow as she stared at Yates's. They were evenly matched, only a few hairs between them.

Dylan sat beside him but didn't speak much. Rick was elsewhere having dinner with his friends and family. Yates imagined that was the reason for Dylan's struck puppy expression. A hint of disappointment had hit Yates too.

If Rick had joined them, Yates would've demanded the seat opposite and kicked his knee caps in under the table, but instead, he was stuck with Aunt Margret and Dylan beside him, yo-yoing his eyebrows and looking as if he might cry.

"You should've seen Sara on the hen night," Hannah howled.

Yates couldn't remember their names, but *Sara* bowed forward, hiding her face in her hands. Yates recognized her as the one who threw up all over the counter in the shop. The one who arrived drunk and left drunker. Being a drunken liability was hilarious apparently.

"You're practically an alcoholic."

Hannah and her friends laughed; even Dylan smiled a little. Yates's expression turned to stone. Sara put her hand up, giggling. "I need to go to AA."

"But after the wedding," Hannah chipped in. "One last hurrah, you need to go all out."

Yates gritted his teeth, glasses clinked, wine trickled. Hannah's friends got louder and louder, pushing the table, shoving back their chairs.

Yates surged to his feet, forcing his lips up into a smile that shook. "This has been a lovely evening. Goodnight."

Not the smoothest of exits, but he didn't care. He owed no one an explanation. Dylan snagged his hand and yanked him. "Don't go."

Yates pulled his hand free and squeezed Dylan's shoulder. He smiled, added a bit of humor into his voice the same way Dylan had in front of Rick. "You stay, enjoy yourself."

"Yates?"

He didn't wait for goodbyes. Yates strolled away, picking up pace once he passed out of view. The restaurant was attached to the hotel, and he took the stairs two steps at a time to get to his and Dylan's room. Twin double beds. No chance of Dylan climbing onto him in the night while asleep.

"Yates!"

He didn't stop at Dylan's shout and didn't turn to him either. "Go back downstairs and enjoy the rest of the meal."

Yates wasn't going to sit around until every member of the bridal party was unable to walk. He wouldn't be carrying any of them to their rooms or turning their heads so they didn't swallow vomit and die. He wouldn't be there when they stirred and threw insults and swinging fists his way. He wouldn't be getting frustrated and shouting about how pathetic they were. He'd been there, done that, signed away twenty years of his life just to escape from it.

"You said you didn't hate me."

"I don't hate you; I'm indifferent."

His chest compressed. His steps faltered, but he pushed on with tunnel vision fixed at their hotel room door. Dylan bounded past and blocked Yates's path.

"Why is it only when I verge on a breakdown that you warm towards me?"

"What?"

Dylan chewed his bottom lip. "Like…when I need you, you've been there for me. I know you find it hard, but you've helped. You've been amazing."

"What's your problem then?"

"That I don't always need you. Sometimes I want you. I want you to be warm without me having to fall to pieces first. Like you were in the shop. You made me a space, you talked to me, we ate lunch together. It was nice, but then it changed." Dylan crowded closer. "I know finding out about…it made you think less of me."

"It wasn't finding out that made me think less of you."

Dylan's eyes widened. "Then what?"

Push past, refuse to answer, go into the room. Dylan would only follow, and they both had key cards to the door. Yates exhaled a long breath through his nose.

"It was your reaction to *us.*"

"What do you mean?"

"You downplayed us in front of Rick. You made it sound like it meant nothing, and so that's what I'm doing. If nothing is what you want, nothing's what you get."

He tried to get by, but Dylan sidestepped in front of him.

"I don't want nothing."

Yates rolled his eyes. "I know exactly what, or should I say who, you want."

Christ, he sounded hysterical.

"After I told you everything, I felt like a weight had gone. I felt free. I could concentrate in my lectures, laugh and joke with my friends. Finish my assignments. I even beat a pot with a spoon as my flatmates jammed with their guitars."

"Is this going somewhere?"

"I was happy. I hadn't even realized I'd been faking happiness as much as I had until I felt it again."

"You don't look very happy."

Dylan swallowed. "Because I know I've messed it up with you. You don't want me anymore after you found out what I've done, the person I am. I told you I was a bad person, and you didn't believe me."

"You're not a bad person."

"I don't want nothing with you, Yates." He slipped his hands up the side of Yates's face and held him.

Why *wasn't* he snapping his wrists, kneeing his stomach?

Why *was* he closing his eyes and lowering his shoulders?

"I need you," Dylan whispered. "That goes without saying, but I want you too. I want you and not him."

"Don't."

"Please, Yates."

Motherfucker.

Dylan pushed up on the tips of his toes and kissed Yates on the mouth. It was a bad idea, the worst idea, but he leaned his head down to receive more of Dylan's gentle kisses.

Why were they so intoxicating? He didn't understand it. This man could leave him breathless. Twenty-one, a drama student, cried a lot. How the hell did he take out Yates's lungs and jab a knife at his heart.

Yates pulled his mouth away. "You've got to go back downstairs."

"Why?"

"I didn't bring any toys with me."

"What?"

Yates licked his lips. He groaned at the taste of Dylan. This was bad. *So bad.* "If we go into this room, we're gonna end up fucking."

No toys or restraints, but fucking. Just fucking. Yates couldn't think of anything worse.

"Good," Dylan whispered against his lips.

That was worse. Yates's whole body shuddered as heat surged through his veins. He plunged his tongue deep into Dylan's mouth and cradled the back of his head. Dylan held his other hand and joined their fingers together.

Yates tugged him in the opposite direction, away from their hotel room. Go back downstairs. *Don't do this.*

"Please, I need this. I want this."

Dylan kissed him softly, and he was weak to it. He pulled Yates the other way, and he followed in a daze, knowing what would happen on the other side of the hotel door but powerless to stop it.

****

Toys and restraints gave the illusion of control. In reality, Yates's secret barrier. They were his defense, his last stand, and they'd always protected him. He wielded pleasure and pain with a thin shield. He dominated and took control, no emotions involved. Devices and aggression. No one got close. No one got skin to skin. That's how he liked it.

Fucking with nothing but sweaty skin sliding and groping hands destroyed his carefully crafted barriers. Dylan burned them to the ground. He made Yates fully lose himself, more than his body, but his emotions too. He kissed Dylan without control, sloppy and wet as they both lost themselves in desire. It was too much, but he couldn't stop stroking and kissing and sliding their wet bodies together. Yates could've kissed him for hours. He could've come from their cocks touching. He was pretty sure one of them had, with the extra slip and slide, but couldn't tell who.

The lips and hands and cocks all felt orgasmic.

"Let me fix your hands to the bed."

Yates begged the words into Dylan's throat.

He had a tie that went with his suit. The bedframe was metal, a bar in the middle looked perfect to pin Dylan's hands above his head. He could still get the situation under some semblance of control.

"No," Dylan gasped. "I want to touch you. It's turning me on so much. I'm high with it."

Yates knew the feeling.

Dylan's fingers brushed down Yates's back; they clutched and stroked and pinched the skin as their cocks ground together. Dylan touched the burns on his body, unbothered by the rough skin and the hard patches.

Yates kissed his way down Dylan's body and moved out of reach of those hands. Dylan could only reach his hair. He gripped on tight, tingling Yates's scalp.

Dylan yanked his hair harder as Yates ran his mouth over his stomach, through his strawberry-scented mound of hair to the base of his cock. He took hold of Dylan, and when the taste hit his tongue, he projected a lustful moan onto Dylan's tip.

"Fuck, Yates..."

He groaned and flung his head back against the pillow. The huffs and gasps of Dylan above trying to hold on lit Yates up inside. They spurred him on. He gripped the base of Dylan's cock in both hands and dropped his mouth down. Dylan squirmed. His legs shook. The pleasurable groans leaving him were sounding more and more like words, bit off curses, and pleas meant for God.

Yates used his lips over Dylan's tip, mouthing at it, sucking on it lightly. He traced the tip of his tongue along the crown before dragging over the top.

He stole the taste from Dylan each time it appeared, rolling his tongue through it, moaning against it.

Dylan tasted good, too good. It got sharper, stronger, thicker. Yates knew he was close. He could feel his pulse jolting through him. Dylan flattened himself against the mattress, tensing all of his trembling muscles. He was peaking, the delicious moment right before you come. Yates pulled his hands down on Dylan's cock and sucked him deep past his lips.

"Oh, fuck, Yates…"

Cum rushed down Yates's throat, coating his mouth. He relaxed, taking it down, breathing through his nose as he swallowed around Dylan's cock.

"I can't wait anymore; I need you to fuck me."

Yates released his cock with a dirty pop and breathed in the scent of strawberries as Dylan twisted his hips. He reached for his jeans hanging from the bed, growling with effort. A look of triumph lit up his face when he found his wallet. Dylan yanked it free, flipped it open, and removed a condom and a packet of lube.

"Who were they meant for?"

Dylan paused, then tore into the wrapper. "You. Only you."

A voice in Yates's head snickered. He knew Dylan lied; he'd been lying to his sister for a year.

"Yates…" He stroked Yates's cheek, never seeing the scars, only seeing deep into Yates's eyes. "I promise."

He nodded, taking the condom from Dylan's fingers. Dylan licked his lips as he watched Yates roll it over his cock. He grabbed Yates's hand, stopping him from going further. Second thoughts.

"I want to do it."

Oh.

His heart nearly ceased to beat. Dylan took over and rolled the condom all the way. He opened the lube and smothered Yates's cock with it while staring into his eyes. This was intimate, too intimate. The eye contact put a flush through Yates's skin.

"I've been practicing with the annihilator," Dylan whispered. "I didn't want to ruin it if we ever got this far."

"How could you possibly ruin this?"

Yates was more in danger of ruining everything. His heart skipped and tripped closer to a heart attack the further they got.

"If it hurt, we'd have to stop. I didn't want to disappoint you."

"Why do you care what I think? This is about your pleasure."

Dylan snorted softly. "This is about so much more than our pleasure. You know it is."

Yates didn't deny it. He took the lube from Dylan, covered his fingers, and pushed one into Dylan's arse. He hissed and tensed up. A bead of sweat ran down his face. Yates worked his finger in and out before adding another, loosening the tight ring of muscle.

"You'll be gentle with me…this time?"

This time? Yates shivered.

"It'll hurt when I first push in."

Dylan's eyes sprang wide open. They searched Yates's.

"I'll go slow. If it ever gets to be too much—"

"Say red, I know."

Red? A safe word. A small barrier to cling to.

Yates shook his head. "No. Tell me to stop, tell me what you don't like, and what you do. I'll listen, I promise."

He guided his cock towards Dylan's hole and pressed on the rim. Dylan's body fought against him, his eyes grew glassy, and he bit his lip in pure frustration, but Yates knew it was coming. The delicious pop as the muscle lost its fight and let him in. Dylan jolted at the sudden give and grabbed onto Yates's shoulder.

"Relax." Yates nuzzled his ear. "Don't be disappointed if you don't come the first time."

He sank deeper into Dylan and watched pain flicker over his face. When he stopped, Dylan's tight features softened. He gazed up at Yates. "It's not about coming. It was never about coming. It was this."

Being full, and pinned, and pushed into over and over, Yates remembered. He remembered it all, and as he rocked his hips into Dylan, he told him how amazing he felt, how tight and hot. Euphoria sparkled in Dylan's eyes, and he looked at Yates with a slack mouth as he poured praise onto him.

"Fuck me, Yates, fuck me."

He bucked, and pleaded, and panted so harshly his mouth went dry. Yates made it wet again with his tongue, gazing down at Dylan as he got off to being pinned and fucked. He kept a tight rein on himself, not going crazy like the feral part of him wanted to.

Yates replaced all Dylan's doubt with fire and fireworks. He smoothed Dylan's lips with his own as he released inside him. The orgasm branched out and filled his head with happy endorphins. Dylan hadn't come his first time, but he smiled and basked in the afterglow like he had.

Yates turned his pleased smile into a gasp, jerking him off until cum splashed onto his sweaty chest. Dylan sighed as Yates licked him clean. His filthy kink of strawberries and cream. There was so much cum on Dylan's chest his tongue started to go numb.

"That was amazing," Dylan groaned.

"It'll get better," Yates said, climbing up the bed. "I'll make it so good you come from one stroke of my cock inside you."

"One stroke?"

Yates nodded. "I'll get you so worked up, tease you until you scream. Then I'll pin you to the bed and fill you up. You'll come with one stroke of me going deep, nice and slow, dragging the length of me over your prostate."

Dylan's eyes fluttered. "I can't wait."

Yates chuckled and ruffled his hair.

"No, I mean it. I can't wait. Let's do it now."

Dylan rolled onto his side, wincing as he did. Yates grabbed his shoulder and kept him still. "You need to give your body a rest for now."

Dylan shot him a sulky face, then mumbled, "We can mess around in a bit, though, right?"

"What do you have in mind?"

"Well..."

He reached down and grabbed Yates's cock still in the dirty condom.

"I haven't tried sucking you off yet."

Yates wasn't going to say no to that...

CHAPTER TWELVE

The morning of the wedding, aka the morning of the contract killing. Yates buttoned up his shirt and slipped on his tie. Dylan did a double-take, frowning at Yates's choice of shirts.

"No flowers?"

"Didn't want to outshine the bride."

Dylan laughed and slid into Yates's arms as if it were the most natural place to be.

"My tongue still aches," he murmured.

Yates snorted. "I told you I've got control."

"You played dirty."

"How?"

Dylan pushed off from his chest. "I was only allowed to lick, lick until you come."

"And you did it…eventually."

"I did."

He shot Yates another pleased smile, just like he had when Yates had finally erupted in his face. Dylan had strained his tongue and had a slight lisp when he said certain words.

"Good job I've not got a speech later."

"What was that?"

Dylan slapped his arm. "Stop it. You know exactly what I said."

He bit his lip. "About tonight…"

"I'll be back in the room before you even wake up."

"What if something happens?"

"Ranger is with me."

"Ranger? He's a softy."

Yates laughed. "Not when he's having one of his 'red' moments. There is no one I'd trust with my life more than Ranger. We'll be fine."

"But—"

"No buts," Yates said, kissing him on the mouth.

Dylan's phone vibrated on the bedside table, and he peeled himself away from Yates.

"Probably Hannah saying she's got a hangover."

"Probably," Yates muttered.

The joy in Dylan's face seeped away as he read the message. Yates side-eyed Dylan as he slipped on his suit. His gut told him who the message was from, and he waited for Dylan to confirm his suspicions. He didn't. Dylan typed something back, pocketed his phone, and said nothing.

"Everything okay?" Yates asked.

Dylan hummed as he nodded. "Yeah. I've still got to get ready; I'll meet you in the lobby."

"Dismissing me, Dylan?"

"Of course not."

Yates was about to question him, but his own phone vibrated in his pant pocket. He pulled it out and frowned at the message from Ranger.

I have a surprise for you downstairs. X

"Everything okay?" Dylan asked.

Yates put his phone away. "Ranger's got a surprise for me downstairs apparently."

"What is it?"

"It wouldn't be a surprise if he told me, would it?"

Dylan snorted. "Point taken."

"I better go see." He strolled to the door, but Dylan leapt across the room and took hold of his arm.

"It was a message from Rick."

Yates stiffened. "What did it say?"

"He asked if I'd meet him."

"So you thought you'd send me away and invite him up."

"No." Dylan scrunched up his face. "I can see why you'd think that, but no. I told him no. Look."

Dylan released Yates's arm and showed his phone. Sure enough, Dylan had texted back no. As Yates scrolled, he saw all the messages from Rick over the past few days, nonstop messages Dylan hadn't replied to. He let out a sigh and handed back the phone.

"Sorry, okay?" Dylan whispered. "I didn't want to bring him up. Today's going to be awkward enough as it is. I wanted this room to be a no-Rick zone."

"It had better stay that way."

"I'll be ready in ten minutes. Meet you downstairs?"

Yates nodded and left Dylan to it. He pushed Dylan and Rick to the back of his mind and brought the contract killing to the front of it. What the hell had Ranger brought to the hotel?

He stopped halfway down the stairs when he saw a familiar face leaning against the desk. Donnie's lips twitched, then spread with a confident smile.

"You should see your face." He laughed.

Sculptured and styled in his tight jeans and a white T-shirt. No bags under his eyes or grease dripping from gangly hair. He looked good, but Yates still marched up to him and shook him by the T-shirt.

"What the hell are you doing here?"

Donnie smiled through the manhandling. "Ranger said you two needed help. I've come to offer my expertise."

"We don't need your help."

"Well, I'm here now. I brought the stuff, and Ranger says he'll ride up on his bike after his brunch da—"

"Get in your car and go."

Donnie laughed. "Don't pretend you're not at least a little bit happy to see me."

"I'm not at all."

Yates thought about punching the pout off Donnie's face, but members of the bridal party were descending the stairs and throwing them curious looks.

Yates let go of Donnie's T-shirt, and he looked down at the creases. "Damn it, Yates. I ironed this on the hood of my car an hour ago."

"You're supposed to be lying low. Please tell me Elliot's hidden away somewhere."

Donnie clacked his tongue. "The thing about that is…" He looked over Yates's shoulder, and sure enough Elliot stood there, grinning ear to ear. His blond hair was a mess of tangles, and there were visible hickeys down his neck.

"What the fuck?"

"I know, right?" Donnie chuckled. "I drove halfway here before realizing he was hiding in the back."

Yates pulled his hair. "You should've driven back."

"Nah, I pulled over, gave him a bit of a punishment at the side of the road—"

"Which was humiliating," Elliot said as he swaggered closer.

"Quit complaining. We were covered by trees; no one could see us."

"That squirrel did. The poor thing dropped his nuts."

Donnie wriggled his eyebrows. "His mouth dropped when he saw bigger ones."

Yates released his hair and held up his hands. "Have you both completely lost it?"

"Relax," Elliot said. "No one saw us."

"There are people who can see you now."

"Oh yeah." Elliot turned around and waved at Dylan's Aunt leaving the elevator.

"You should be in hiding."

Donnie sighed. "We can't stay in hiding forever, and we've taken precautions."

"Like what?"

"Elliot now goes by a different name."

"Which is?"

"Eli."

"Christ." Yates spun away. "It's not a joke. If Marc Russo finds out he's alive…"

"He won't," Elliot said.

Donnie nodded. "Besides, you need our help."

"I don't—"

"Okay, let me rephrase. Ranger needs our help with you."

"What?"

"He's worried about you, and the fact you haven't pummeled me into the floor has me worried about you too."

Yates got in Donnie's face. "There are people around."

"That hasn't stopped you trying before."

Elliot knocked into Yates's side and spoke through half of his mouth. "Who's cute, with big freckles and coming this way?"

"Dylan…" Yates turned around.

Dylan stopped in front of them, suited up and ready to go.

"This is Ranger's surprise?" Dylan asked.

He darted looks between Elliot and Donnie as a blush began forming on his cheeks.

"As you can see, I'm not happy about it," Yates said.

"There's no guarantee a surprise will be a happy one." Donnie winked at Yates, then extended his hand out to Dylan. "I'm Donnie. I've heard a lot about you."

Dylan shook his hand while smiling at Yates. "Really?"

"Not from him, but Ranger. Ranger's told me a lot about you and Yates."

"Ranger knows nothing," Yates growled.

Elliot shook Dylan's hand too. "I'm Donnie's fiancé."

Donnie smirked. "No, you're not."

"His husband then."

"I like the sound of that, but still no."

Elliot stuck out his bottom lip. "Fine, I'm his partner and Yates's failure."

Dylan frowned, searching Yates's face for clues. "Your failure?"

"He couldn't kill me and ended up saving me in the end."

"I was saving Donnie. You were just…there."

Elliot grinned. "Now we're best mates too."

"Not on your life."

Yates wrapped his arm around Dylan's waist.

Donnie and Elliot both gaped before looking at each other.

"That's a new development." Donnie snorted.

"What is?" Dylan asked.

"Yates has his arm around someone, and it's not to break their ribs."

"We've got a wedding to get to," Yates said. "Don't be here when I get back."

He led Dylan away but still managed to hear Donnie call out after them.

"We will be. Have fun, lovebirds."

****

"Your friends seem nice."

It was the first thing Dylan had said since they'd taken their seats in the ceremony room.

Yates snorted. "They're idiots."

"But you're not denying their friends."

"Surprised I have more than a comatose one?"

"No. You've got Ranger too… Did you visit your friend in the hospital?"

Yates shook his head. "No. I've called for updates. Edna's hanging on."

"You should go see her."

"No, been there, done that. It's not a pleasant experience."

Dylan frowned. "What do you mean?"

Yates didn't answer.

"I was thinking…I've got a play coming up—"

"I'm not reading lines with you."

Dylan laughed. "No, I wasn't gonna ask that. I wanted to know if…"

"Yes?"

"If maybe …"

"Spit it out."

"You'll come see it? See me?"

Hell no, that was Yates's immediate response, but then he looked at Dylan's eyes, and his teeth mauling his bottom lip while he waited for Yates's reply.

"Yes."

Short, and to the point. That one word brightened Dylan's face, and he held Yates's gaze until warmth fed through into his cold heart and he had to look away.

"Yeah?"

"I said so, didn't I?"

Dylan nodded, still grinning. "I can't wait."

The backdoors of the ceremony room opened, and Rick strolled inside, fidgeting with his cufflinks. He pointedly didn't look at Yates and Dylan despite them being sat in the front row. His blush pink tie and handkerchief matched the flowers and balloons around the room.

Too pale and washed out for Yates's preference.

Dylan caught him evil-eyeing the closest lot of flowers. "What do you think of the color scheme?"

Blush pink, pastel pink, and white.

"Painfully ordinary."

Dylan laughed. Rick flashed him a look. Dylan didn't notice, but Yates did.

"I think the colors are pretty."

"It's funny how people worry about the trivial things. The colors, the flowers, the menu, the cake, and then still end up marrying arseholes. I guess they do say love is blind."

Dylan met Yates's eyes and smiled. Despite not wanting to, Yates ended up smiling too.

"When I saw you, I fell in love, and you smiled because you knew."

Yates's heart stopped in his chest. He broke their eye contact.

What the hell was that?

"It's a Shakespeare quote," Dylan said. He ducked his head. "Drama student, remember?"

Yates's heart fluttered back to life.

He snorted, then fell serious, catching Dylan's eyes again.

"If you live to be a hundred, I want to live to be a hundred minus one day, so I never have to live without you."

Dylan swallowed. "Who said that?"

"Winnie the Pooh."

Dylan burst out laughing, then stifled his mouth with his hand. Rick glanced over again, no longer neutral but angry. His jaw ticked, and his nostrils flared.

Everyone began getting to their feet. Dylan stood up, still snorting under his hand. Yates glared at Rick, and he turned to face the front of the room, awaiting his bride.

Dylan's hand dropped from his mouth as he gasped. "Hannah…"

Hannah made her way down the aisle with the biggest grin Yates had ever seen. Her eyes sparkled, and she vibrated with glee as she took in all her guests, last of all her brother. Hannah's brow twitched, and she fanned her hand in front of her face as if trying not to cry. Dylan's eyes swelled with tears, and he gripped Yates's hand and squeezed it until Yates's knuckles popped.

Hannah's dress needed a two-meter clearance, and the train that dragged on the floor seemed endless. She got to the front, and Rick kissed her cheek and whispered something into her ear that released a tear from her lashes. She wiped it away as she beamed up at him.

It was all too sickly sweet for Yates, and he couldn't stop the eye roll.

Dylan pinched him. "Behave."

Yates stopped listening when the vicar began droning on. There was soft music, a murmured prayer, lots of tears from Hannah, and then the line Yates had been waiting for.

"If anyone knows just cause why this man and this woman may not be joined together in holy matrimony, let them speak now or else forever hold their peace."

Dylan squeezed his hand so hard the tips of Yates's fingers turned blue. Yates looked at him. Wondering whether he'd save his sister from an arsehole or go through with his plan for a fantasy happily ever after. Air wheezed in and out of his nose, his eyes were fixed on his sister, and his lips were pressed tightly together, holding in any protests.

"Let us continue."

Dylan bowed forward and released the breath he'd been holding to his shoes.

"Wait…"

Motherfucker.

Yates widened his eyes and gaped at Rick. He stepped away from Hannah and held his hands up to stop her from coming any closer. "Wait, I can't."

Hannah shook her head. "What…what do you mean?"

Gasps and grumbles travelled through the guests. Dylan looked at Yates, then back at the unfolding drama.

"I can't do this," Rick said.

He took another step away from Hannah, closer to Dylan. Yates crushed Dylan's hand as Dylan began to loosen his death grip.

This wasn't happening.

Tears rushed down Hannah's face. "What do you mean you can't do this?"

"I'm sorry."

Rick turned and ran down the aisle. The gasps and murmurs turned to anger and outrage. Hannah dropped to her knees as she released a heart-splitting sob. Her bridesmaids rushed around her, shielding her with their blush pink dresses.

Yates stood side by side with Dylan. No murmurs or gasps came from them. Yates's hand shook as he tried to keep his grip on Dylan.

"Let go of my hand," Dylan whispered.

Yates swallowed the nails in his throat. "No."

"Yates."

"I won't."

He couldn't.

Dylan turned his head. His eyes burned into the side of Yates's face. The noise in the room, the commotion, all seemed to fade. Yates could only focus on Dylan despite not being able to face him.

"Red."

The one remaining heartstring in Yates's chest twanged as it snapped. Not a string. But sharp wire that tore as it broke away. A safe word. Dylan had thrown up a shield, a barrier, a distance between them. He'd broken down Yates's walls, flung himself into Yates's grasp before cruelly pulling himself away.

Yates released his hand, and Dylan bolted. He didn't rush to his sister surrounded by her friends, wailing for her broken heart. He turned away from her and fought the guests piling into the aisle. Dylan went after Rick without once looking back at Yates or his broken sister drowning in despair.

A numbness swept over Yates as he left his chair. Elbows and arms knocked into him as he walked the aisle, but he didn't growl, or curse, or threaten the clumsy guests around him. He couldn't. There was nothing inside, not even his old friend anger. Just emptiness.

He couldn't even conjure up murderous hatred toward Rick. His heartbreak wasn't down to him. It was Yates's responsibility. He should never have allowed Dylan to punch his fist through his chest and grasp that last damning heartstring.

The first time he met Dylan, he should've kicked him out of the shop or done as Dylan asked.

He should've killed him.

Killed him.

Killed.

That was all that could bring feeling back to his chest. A well-worked plan. A successful campaign. A win. Dylan, his shredded heart, the wedding, they were nothing, some damning detour he shouldn't have taken.

He wasn't some flower shop man who fell in love. He was a strategist and an assassin.

Bloodthirsty and savage using his shop as a decoy.

When had it ever been about flowers?

Or emotions?

Or fucking love?

A growl vibrated in Yates's throat as he left the ceremony room.

Mr Stevenson was about to die, sooner than planned.

CHAPTER THIRTEEN

Donnie strolled over with his usual swagger until he got a good look at Yates and rushed the last few strides. "What happened?"

"Keys," Yates said.

Donnie fished them out of his pocket and slapped them down on Yates's palm. He turned away, heading in the direction of the hotel parking lot.

"Hey..." Donnie grabbed his arm, but Yates threw him off and shoved him in the chest. Donnie stumbled back, watching Yates with wary eyes.

"Back off."

Donnie didn't listen. He followed behind, keeping a distance in case Yates lashed out again. He wanted to swing for Donnie, but he wanted to batter Mr Stevenson bloody more.

"You're back from the wedding early..."

Yates gritted his teeth. "Go find Elliot and run off into the sunset together."

"Not yet, we've got a job to do."

"There's no *we*. I'm doing it myself."

Donnie laughed at him, and Yates whirled around with his fist at the ready. It slapped the laugh from Donnie's face, and he stiffened, raising his hands slowly. They faced off against each other, two beasts prepared to claw and bite to win.

"I don't want to fight," Donnie whispered.

"Then leave me alone."

"Ranger talked me through the plan. Eight guards. One target. You can't do it alone. It's suicide."

"As long as I kill him first, it doesn't matter. I'll kill him. I have to."

"This isn't like you."

"What isn't?"

Donnie lowered his hands and relaxed his stance. "Acting all crazy."

"Why do you and Ranger get to act crazy, but I don't?"

"We need one of us sane to stay alive."

"Not me. Not this time."

Yates got to the car and opened up the trunk. Guns, knives, flashbangs, smoke grenades. Donnie's and Ranger's weapons of choice, but not his. He'd kill Mr Stevenson with his bare fucking hands.

"Where's Dylan?"

"I don't give a shit about Dylan!"

Donnie grunted. "I didn't ask whether you gave a shit. I asked where he was."

Yates slammed the trunk down and didn't answer.

"This is mad. Ranger will be here soon. You can't go off alone."

"Are you going to stop me?"

"What?"

Yates fixed him with a glare. "Are you going to stop me? You're gonna have to take out my kneecaps to stop me, Donnie. You're gonna have to break my goddamn legs."

"I'll stand in front of the car."

"And I'll drive through you." Yates stabbed his finger out at Donnie. "Don't you get it? You mean nothing. You and Ranger are nothing to me. I don't care about you. I don't care about anyone except Mr fucking Stevenson. Now go find Elliot, and leave me alone!"

Yates moved around the side of the car and flung open the door. He got in and started the engine. Donnie walked away, and Yates thought they were done, but when he tried to exit the parking lot, Donnie stood in front of the barrier. It lifted behind him, but he crossed his arms, flexed his jaw, and didn't move.

Yates wound down the window. "Move."

"No."

"I swear to God, Donnie—"

"What do you swear, huh?"

"I'll drive through you."

Donnie lifted his chin and presented Yates with his cockiest grin. "Why haven't you then?"

Yates revved the engine, staring Donnie down, who only fluttered his eyelashes in response.

Bastard.

"Donnie!"

Elliot dropped the two coffee cups he was holding and gaped at Yates threatening to run Donnie down. His eyes were round and glassy and Yates saw the exact moment the look sliced into Donnie's chest. The same way Dylan could disarm him, Elliot could do to Donnie.

Elliot beckoned Donnie towards him, and he shifted an inch.

"I didn't save you so you could be an idiot," Yates shouted. "You have something more, Donnie. I don't. This is the only thing I've got, don't take it from me. I don't want or need you to. This is what I want, and him over there is what you want, so go get him."

"Get out of the way!" Elliot screamed.

Donnie flinched. "Not until Yates calms down and tells me what's going on."

"I'm going to count down from three. If you don't move, I swear I'll run you down."

"I don't believe it."

"Three."

"Don't!" Elliot ran out and crashed into Donnie's chest.

Exactly what Yates expected would happen because Elliot fucking loved Donnie, and the horror on Donnie's face said he loved Elliot too.

"Two."

Donnie bared his teeth at Yates. He shook with rage with his hands around Elliot, attempting to push him clear, but he clung on like some bleach-blond koala.

"One."

He slammed his foot down on the gas, not blinking as he hurtled towards Donnie and Elliot. Donnie pulled Elliot aside, and they both crashed down on the concrete as Yates zipped by them.

Elliot was Donnie's weakness. He would never allow Elliot to get hurt, would lose every time if Elliot was on the line. Some would've said it was sweet, romantic, but not Yates.

He looked back at them through the mirror. Donnie had pulled Elliot to his feet and was patting him down. Yates smirked as bitterness churned in his gut. "So pathetic."

Love was poison. He'd flushed it from his system once, and he was going to do it again.

****

Yates stared at the house with all the burning hatred he possessed. Ranger had suggested they scale the cliff, but after an aerial inspection, Yates knew it wasn't possible. The cliff wasn't just sheer but made from white chalk, crumbly and hazardous.

A tall wall surrounded the house with rings of razor wire glinting in the sun. The only way in was through the gate, and Yates spied three guards. Two huddled together sharing a smoke, one standing tall, surveying the landscape as if he knew Yates hid in the hedgerow.

He'd left the car way behind him, covering it in bushes and foliage, before creeping his way to the property. He'd had to crawl, dragging the heavy rucksack on his back. The deconstructed rifle swung into his hip as if reminding him he wasn't the best man to use it.

Ranger would've found himself a good spot and taken as many guards out as he could. There were plenty of high trees to choose from. That was the original plan, but Donnie had strutted into proceedings, and despite Yates being pissed at him being there, he couldn't help but plan.

Donnie would've used the rifle; Ranger would've come with Yates to the gate. Ranger, who was better at close-quarters fighting, was practically invincible when he got in a rage. The handguns and knives were better suited to him.

There was no point assigning roles to Donnie and Ranger; they weren't there. It was all on him.

Yates growled under his breath. If he shot with the rifle from that distance, he'd never get close enough to take down the gate, but crawling up to the guards and kissing their boots wasn't an option either. They'd trigger the alarm and blow out the back of his head.

His phone buzzed in his pocket, but Yates cut off Ranger's call and set his phone to busy. Unlike Ranger and Donnie, Yates's strongest weapon was his phone, or more specifically the information he had on it. Deadly information. This was his forte, his tool, his answer.

He'd spent weeks gathering it all together.

Yates typed out a message, attached a few damning photographs courtesy of his client, and pressed send. He shifted as he took up the binoculars once again and observed the guards he'd texted.

Justin Kelly, Harry Seinfeld, Vince Sharp. He'd identified them as soon as he saw them. Seth had found the names, and Jeromy had found information on them. Yates sorted through to find the relevant pieces to use. Nine times out of ten, that meant family. Loved ones were a weakness. Justin's daughter had only been born four months ago, baby Eva, two weeks early, emergency C-section. His third child. He had Samuel and Ella, aged eight and five. They loved their new little sister. Yates Knew Harry Seinfeld's boys were both soccer lovers. He knew Vince Sharp and his wife went through one hell of an IVF struggle to be blessed with their daughter, Hope. All three guys had weaknesses Yates could exploit, and those weaknesses were going to save their lives.

Justin read the message first. He threw his cigarette onto the floor, not bothering to stamp it out. Yates could see his frown, his face of disgust as he tilted his phone towards Harry. They both stared. Harry pulled away and retrieved his phone, looking over the damning images for himself.

He called for Vince, who was reluctant to give up his vigil over the fields. He knew a beast stalked them, a beast waited, but Yates didn't want to sink his teeth into them. He wanted them to walk free and sacrifice the monster inside the house.

Vince checked his own phone, gaping with the same horror as his colleagues. Yates put down the binoculars and sent another message. More stomach-churning photographs, of young boys and girls being abused by the man inside the house, the man they were being paid to protect.

The photographs had been given to him as a reason, not a payment. Kill Mr Stevenson because of this, because of what he's done, what he did to me. *Lily.*

Her voice had broken, tears had fuzzed her eyes, and for a moment she'd looked lost in her head, in the hell inside it he'd put there. It'd only eased when Yates had said he'd make Mr Stevenson pay, eased, but not faded altogether. The thought of his death made her lips twitch into a cruel smile. Yates had liked that look; he'd responded to it with his own sharp expression. He got pleasure from money, sex, flowers, but rarely a hit. This one excited him.

People like Mr Stevenson, your employer, deserve to die.

They agreed with him. Yates knew they did by the looks on their faces. Disgust, revulsion, anger. Harry shuddered and slapped his hand over his mouth.

These children had parents, had loving families, had futures. They were innocent.

Yates only met one of the children, one kept by one of the monsters in the photographs, toyed with and abused until she got too old and he craved fresh meat. He let her go into the world wild and angry, broken and shamed, until she found the strength to carve out a life for herself. To enjoy the simple things. The sunshine on her skin, flowers in bloom, the swish of trees in the wind, and the twinkle of starlight. She found a reason to keep on going, but many didn't.

Unlock the gate, put your guns on the floor, and walk left until you hit the road. If you don't, I'll see it as a sign you condone this disgusting monster. I'll see it as a sign you're like him, and I'll kill you too. You have thirty seconds to decide.

He nodded at his message and pressed send. They'd all messaged his number, but he didn't reply to them. They had to decide what kind of men they were, what kind of fathers. What kind of humans.

Would they stand and protect a pedophile? The man who made those pictures and sold children to the highest bidder? The man who destroyed childhoods and damaged minds beyond all recognition? Who brought pain and tears and allowed grown men to get off on that?

Harry put down his gun first. Yates had been watching them talk through the binoculars. The men went back and forth, snappy and snarling, but a lot of the anger was directed at the house. Harry decided, and they stopped arguing. He walked away, shaking his head, and Justin jogged to join him.

Vince didn't move. Stress lined his face; he gripped his hair and stared directly at Yates. For a moment he wondered whether the binoculars were reflecting the sun at him, blinking to let him know he wasn't crazy. Yates was close by and gagging for a kill.

Vince looked at the gate, contemplating. He typed out a message on his phone. At first, Yates wasn't going to check it, but curiosity picked at him, and he looked, deflating with a sigh as he ran his thumb over the numbers.

457823

The code to get in. Who needed guns and knives when you had a phone full of information? Vince ran to catch up with his colleagues. They kept walking, not looking back until they passed through the first row of trees, disappearing into green fields. It would be a mile until they met the road, but the gunshots would still carry to them. They'd know. Yates hoped it would make them smile.

Three guards down out of eight. There were cameras around the property, but it didn't take much for Yates to find the company and the system. Then it was all about finding the right person to take them out. Yates typed out another message, and this time he waited for the reply, huffing at the thumbs up.

Don't confirm with a goddamn emoji.

Yates left the bulky rifle and the rounds that went with it and continued in a crouch. Five guards. He reasoned some would be inside the property, and others prowling the grounds. At some point, they'd notice the naked gate, and Yates wanted to be there for it.

His phone buzzed; he looked down at Dylan's name and felt a boulder drop into the bottom of his stomach. He itched to answer but didn't, and like he'd done with Ranger and Donnie, he muted the call and took off in a crouched jog towards the gate.

He kept off the driveway and slowed his pace as he approached the wall. Eight-foot, ten inches thick, barely a scratch or a scuff. The curls of razor wire looked brand new, and Yates's research had confirmed it, installed only a week ago, ready for him.

It was a challenge. Kill me if you can.

Footsteps twisted up gravel on the other side of the gate.

"The cameras are down."

Yates grunted and took his first step onto the loose stones. He made his way to the wall and pressed his back to it as he edged closer to the keypad.

"Hey, did you hear me?"

457823

Yates grunted as he typed in the code.

"Why are your guns on the ground?"

The gate made a grinding sound as it opened. Yates didn't move. He waited for the guard to come to him. As soon as he put himself in Yates's line of sight, he had him. Yates used his forearm to pin the guard against the wall, who struggled and panted.

Eren Bell. Young. As young as Dylan. His eyes watered, and his lip wobbled. He still lived with his mother, refusing to pay rent according to her social media page. Eren loved his fast cars, expensive clothes, priceless jewelry. A diamond the size of a marble shone in his ear lobe.

"Please don't…"

Yates kept him pinned while disarming him with his other hand. A knife, a handgun, a screwdriver.

"Listen to me very carefully. I want you to walk left and keep walking through the trees until you get to the road. If I see you turn around or stop, I'll—"

"Kill me."

An image of Dylan flashed behind Yates's eyes. He shook it away.

"No, not you, but your mother."

"My…mother?"

"8 Fields Way, Harlow. That's where you live together."

"Yeah, how did you—"

"I've got a man waiting, gun at the ready." Yates hummed as he checked the time on his phone. "It's just after two. Your mother will be sitting on the sofa watching Nurse On Call."

It was a bluff but had the desired effect; a tear rushed down Eren's cheek. "How did—"

"Go…"

Yates shoved Eren away. He staggered, still watching Yates with wide, watery eyes, then he took off in a sprint.

Four down, and not a shot fired, not a drop of blood spilled. Yates knew it wouldn't last. He gathered up the guns and knives and put them in his rucksack before hauling them onto his shoulder. He didn't need them while his phone was still taking out Mr Stevenson's men with ease.

Another text, another conflicted man. This time, Gareth Simons. His sick mother was all alone in the hospital in Leeds. Yates had found her and made someone pose with a pillow near her head. One photograph only took five seconds, but the impact had Gareth flooring it from the mansion in his car, lashing Yates with stones.

He was the last man to run.

The rest ignored Yates's messages and threats.

They were prepared to die for the arseholes inside the mansion.

Yates pocketed his phone and drew his gun instead.

CHAPTER FOURTEEN

Yates inched his foot out from behind the wall. A shot that rang out blew the brick he leaned by to pieces. Yates growled at the debris in his eyes, shuffling away. They knew he was there. Of course, they did. This was the moment he needed Ranger or Donnie someplace high, covering him as he rushed inside the gate. *Damn it, stop thinking of them.* They weren't there; he was on his own. Like he wanted.

He tried again, and the same result. The bricks exploded by his face. Something hot dripped down his cheek from where a chunk had caught him. It dripped from his chin to his shirt; the blood drops burst through the fibers and reminded him of poppies. Yates kept still and listened to the creep of boots. The gravel gave them away. Yates knew they were coming but didn't know if they were foolish enough to poke their head out.

They weren't.

Yates hissed through his teeth and thought about his options. He was fucked.

"Did you kill them, or did they run?"

The flat tone gave nothing away. Yates responded with his own monotone voice.

"They ran."

"Cowards. I hate cowards."

"Why do you defend one then?"

"The same reason you kill for one. Money."

Yates snorted. "I'm not being paid. I'm doing this for free."

"Doing what exactly? Leaning against a wall, waiting to come inside. You've blown the element of surprise."

"You always knew I was coming."

"Yes." The man sighed. "Mr Stevenson knew you were coming. Finally, he'll be able to relax knowing it happened. You came. You fucked up. I killed you."

Yates grew tired of the back and forth. He itched to test the shooters inside the gate, roll from his hiding space and see how fast they could shoot. One of them was going to die. Why delay the inevitable? At least if Yates failed, he'd be put out of his goddamn misery. He rolled out, only to freeze wide-eyed at the section missing from the guy's face. Blood sprayed into the air like a cartoon, and the only sound to puncture the silence was a squelch from the top of his head and a gurgle from his lips.

The rifle fired again, another guard, another grunt, another shot.

Another frontal lobe blasted into the air with a spray of red. Yates turned from his position on the ground and spied Ranger running, gun in both hands like a man possessed. Shock slowed Yates's mind. Gravel crunched, and he spotted a man, Arnold Barnes, not looking at him sprawled on the ground, but Ranger.

Arnold aimed his gun at Ranger.

Yates lifted his own and shot him again and again. He flailed and jerked as he fell, and Donnie with the rifle—wherever he was— made sure he was dead with a neat shot in his forehead. Arnold went down in specular fashion, a bloody firework display of color.

Yates snorted. Donnie must've been practicing. That was it. They'd killed the last three guards.

Ranger's feet pounded closer. Yates spun towards him with a relieved breath and a hint of a smile, but it dropped from his face. Ranger leapt on him. He took the collar of Yates's shirt in his hands and shook him, cursing, and drooling, and rabid in his anger.

The old Ranger.

He grabbed Yates's throat and squeezed. "Stupid fucker, trying to get yourself killed. You wanna die, I'll kill ya, right here, right now."

Yates slapped his hand, but Ranger didn't relent. "Stupid. Selfish. Evil fucker."

Darkness swept into Yates's vision. His fingers fighting to remove Ranger turned fuzzy. Even his splutter didn't deter Ranger from repeatedly bashing Yates's head into the ground and growling his utter hatred.

A growl broke them apart. Yates spluttered and rolled on his side. His vision swam, but he saw them, two bloodthirsty beasts racing towards them with their ears back and teeth gleaming.

Dogs.

Yates hadn't considered dogs. Max hadn't photographed any dogs.

Ranger lifted his head, the mist in his eyes cleared, and he rolled off Yates, grinning dopily at the two shepherds eating up the distance.

"I fucking love dogs."

They were growling, and frothing, and running flat out. Yates blinked, swaying his hand out to Ranger to pull him back.

"Ranger." Yates grabbed his arm, but Ranger peeled his fingers away like they were nothing. Yates gaped, still hazy, but unable to look away. He was about to see Ranger's face ripped off, his body punctured and torn to pieces.

Why wasn't Donnie taking them out?

They were too low to the ground for Donnie to see over the wall. He couldn't help them. Ranger stumbled towards the dogs like a toddler drunk at the sight of a sweet shop. Open arms, open smile. His eyes bright with glee.

"Who's a good boy?" Ranger said, slapping his thighs. "Such a good boy."

He dropped to his knees and cooed at the dogs, speaking in a babyish tone. They'd entranced him. Yates grabbed for him, but Ranger punched him in the shoulder, knocking him back to the ground.

"I saw them first. You can pet them second."

Ranger's friendly display threw the dogs off their stride. They skidded to a halt in front of him, still snapping and snarling but without a doubt confused. Yates could sympathize. His mind struggled to compute. *Why weren't they tearing Ranger to pieces?* Why hadn't the scent of blood and the screams of pain escaped into the air?

"Such good boys, aren't you? So big and strong and what lovely tails you have."

Tails? Yates's brain spun. *What the actual fuck?*

Ranger continued to speak weirdly. He lowered himself from his knees to his arse, still speaking to the dogs, cooing at them. One even dared to wag its tail. The other one tilted its head, thoroughly confused. Yates found himself doing the same.

"I've got something for ya." Ranger reached into his pocket, still complimenting the dogs in his childish voice, and pulled out a steak.

A motherfucking steak.

Yates pinched himself, confirming he could still feel. This was happening. He hadn't died after all. Ranger was speaking in baby language while waggling a juicy steak in the dogs' faces.

"Why the hell?"

"You interrupted my lunch date," Ranger said. "Donnie called and I got on my bike. Thought I might need it."

"Need it?"

"Well, it's a good job I've got it, huh?"

Ranger ripped the steak in two and dished it out to the conflicted dogs.

"Such good boys," Ranger told them. "Such expensive taste, fifty-quid steak."

They swallowed their pieces whole. Yates stiffened, preparing for them to launch at Ranger for seconds, but they didn't move. They licked their chops and shifted on their legs. At one point they glanced at each other.

"Come on," Ranger said, getting to his feet. He turned his head and looked at Yates. "I'm talking to you right now."

Yates slowly got to his feet.

"No sudden movements, no running, and we'll be fine. They're taught to chase."

"You're crazy," Yates mumbled. "Motherfucking crazy."

"Sometimes crazy can be useful." He narrowed his eyes at Yates. "Not in your case. Your crazy is just plain stupid. What were you thinking?" Ranger pressed his fingers into his temple. "Actually, don't tell me right now. I'll end up killing you. My vision is compromised with red fog. Let's get your man first."

****

Ranger took the upstairs, and Yates prowled the downstairs. The mansion was quiet except for their careful steps and the occasional whine of a dog. Yates jolted when one pawed on the front door, asking to be let in, no doubt asking to see Ranger.

Mr Stevenson was nowhere to be found.

"Anything?" Yates shouted.

"Nothing. He's got a good hiding spot. Let's burn the place."

Yates shook his head. He didn't want the uncertainty of torching the place. He wanted to know Mr Stevenson was dead. He wanted to see him take his last breath. He wanted to look into his eyes.

"I've called Donnie, told him to bring the car."

"Good."

Ranger bounded down the stairs. "I'll check outside, by the cliff. Maybe he took the coward's way out."

Yates stomach sank. He'd thought that too. Mr Stevenson might have jumped. One peek over the edge, and Yates might have seen his body battered on the rocks below. It would have been a victory, but a hollow one.

Ranger opened the back doors and headed in the direction of the cliffs. The dogs rushed after him, eager to be his shadow. Yates could hear him talking to them, babying them, telling them not to get too close to the edge in case they slipped.

"It's over. Come out."

No response.

"We're gonna torch the house. Wouldn't you prefer a bullet to the head to burning alive?"

A floorboard above creaked. Yates glared at the ceiling. "I'll make it quick."

Another small creak.

Yates trod lightly on his feet as he headed towards the stairs. "You know why I'm here, what you've done. Being shot is a mercy compared to what you put those kids through."

He got to the top of the stairs and fixated on the mirror at the end of the hallway. Usually, he avoided looking at his reflection. The scars and his dead eyes were too much to stomach, but this time he looked, he really looked. The mirror was big; bulky screws fixed it to the wall.

"I know you're there."

He ran his hand along the side of the mirror, sighing at the bumps of hinges. This was it. The moment.

"Come out."

Nothing.

Yates aimed the gun at the mirror, between his loveless eyes. Himself. His biggest enemy. "I can shoot you through it, but there's no guarantee where I'd hit. If you come out, I'll make it quick, practically painless."

He waited. The longest five seconds of his life passed.

A latch clicked. The mirror opened, and Mr Stevenson stepped out. Ashen, old, frail. Not a man you'd look at on sight and think monster. He staggered through the hole in the wall using his cane. His eyes were covered with dark shades, and once he was out, he knocked his cane from side to side to judge his surroundings.

"You'll make it quick," he said, not raising his face to Yates. "Through the head."

"Anything I do will be too quick and too painless."

The door slammed below.

Yates spoke over his shoulder. "I've found him."

"Who sent you? I always knew someone would come for me one day, but I want to know who."

"Lily." Yates stepped closer, gun at the ready.

Mr Stevenson nodded at the name.

"She asked me to kill you."

Mr Stevenson's knuckles were white as he gripped his cane, waiting for the end.

"I remember her. Sweet girl, so trusting." His cracked lips lifted into a smile. "Very popular…"

Yates kneed him in the stomach and let him crumple to the ground. He wheezed and whimpered on the floor, face crinkling with pain. It wasn't enough. It would never be enough. Breaking every bone in his body wouldn't be enough, and in his frail old state, he'd be dead before Yates finished.

Yates straddled Mr Stevenson's skinny form. He stole the sunglasses from his face and slipped them over his eyes.

"Just shoot me and get it over with."

Yate lifted an eyebrow. "Shoot you? I'm not gonna shoot you."

He leaned back and grabbed the cane off the floor. He tried to snap it, but it didn't break. "This will be perfect."

Mr Stevenson wetted his thin lips. "What?"

Yates pressed the cane lengthways against his throat; throwing his body forward, he leaned all his weight on it as Mr Stevenson wriggled. He pressed until blood burst in his eyes, and his Adam's apple collapsed inwards. Yates's arms shuddered as he forced the cane harder, hooking it underneath Mr Stevenson's jaw and applying pressure until his throat caved in. He stayed in that position long after Mr Stevenson's last breath had rattled through his crushed windpipe.

When his lips turned navy and the skin underneath his eyes turned purple, Yates eased off and rested against the wall.

He let his eyes slide shut, but Dylan was on the other side of him. The back of him as he rushed from the venue to be with Rick, not him. That fresh wound continued to bleed, and he had no clue how to fix it.

He swung his head towards the creaking stairs but didn't open his eyes.

"It's done," Yates mumbled. "Is Donnie here yet?"

No answer.

He hated being ignored. Yates opened his eyes. Everything was dark behind the sunglasses, but he blinked in surprise at Eren frozen on the top step. His eyes bulged from his head, and his lip trembled as he took in the sight of Mr Stevenson dead on the floor.

"Get out," Yates said, knocking his head against the wall. "Your mother's fine. Go home."

Eren nodded numbly but didn't retreat. His uncertainty made Yates think of Dylan. He didn't want to think of Dylan. It hurt. It made his chest implode, and the memories of the night before come back. Yates had felt happy, actually happy. He gritted his teeth and squeezed his eyes shut behind the glasses.

Piercing pain exploded in his leg. He sprung his eyes open and twisted from the pain, but it came with him. Eren pulled the screwdriver from his thigh, then lunged, driving red-hot pain through Yates's bicep, followed by his shoulder, getting closer to his neck, his jugular.

Why when he looked at Eren, did he see Dylan? Why was Yates still sitting with his back to the wall, taking it? Deflecting the blows from vital places but letting them come. The screwdriver dug into the wall as it missed. It came at him again and scraped his collarbone. His shoulder. His bicep. He preferred this pain. He could handle this physical one with a sigh, but not the one in his chest. That hurt too much.

"Yates!"

Donnie called for him, ending Eren's frenzy. The wall had been more damaged than Yates, but still, he felt the pain. Blood poured from his body, hot and sticky on his skin.

Donnie's steps pounded the stairs, and instinct alerted Yates to the danger Donnie was walking into.

"Watch out!"

Before Eren had a chance to launch at Donnie with the screwdriver, his brains were leaving him from a messy hole at the back of his head. Eren's body dropped to his knees, revealing a startled Donnie holding his gun.

"Fuck," Donnie said. He called over his shoulder to Ranger, "Stop playing with those dogs and get your arse in here."

Ranger bounded upstairs while complaining, then came to an abrupt stop next to Donnie.

Yates didn't have the energy to snort or sneer. "You've seen me looking worse."

Blood snaked around his arm. It made a puddle on the floor, and yet Ranger and Donnie didn't look at those places. Their eyes were glued to his face, his scarred, ugly face where the screwdriver hadn't touched. The sunglasses hid his eyes, but there was no mistaking the trails on his cheeks. The saltiness of tears touched his lips.

Ranger crouched down in front of him. "You're…you're crying."

He didn't deny it, nor growl and curse at Donnie and Ranger for watching. He closed his eyes, let go of the breath he'd been holding, and mumbled, "I am."

Ranger and Donnie shared a worried glance before moving in unison and each grabbing one of Yates's arms.

"Come on," Ranger said, patting Yates's back. "Let's get you back to your flowers."

****

They helped him into the car before Donnie got out and took the driver's seat. Elliot sat in the passenger seat, chewing gum and flicking through a magazine. He glanced at Yates before looking again and gaping. The gum dropped from his mouth into the footwell.

"You look like you've been—"

"Attacked with a screwdriver? Yes."

Elliot shrugged and popped a fresh piece of gum into his mouth.

"One sec," Ranger said, getting out. The trunk opened, and the car filled with whines and pants.

Donnie frowned through the mirror. "What the hell?"

"I can't leave them."

"They're attack dogs."

"They didn't attack."

Ranger got in next to Yates and looked over the dressings around his body. It had been a patch job, but it had slowed the bleeding. Donnie started the engine and took off. If Yates had had the strength, he would've turned and watched the house fade into the distance. He took off the sunglasses and slipped them into the top pocket of his shirt.

"Anyone else got déjà vu?" Elliot asked.

Donnie turned to him. "What?"

"Déjà vu, but this time it's you and me that saved Yates."

"Does your boy-toy have an off switch?" Yates asked.

Donnie clacked his tongue. "Nope, many, many *on* switches, though."

Elliot laughed and slapped Donnie's thigh. Their love was painful to watch, and Yates averted his gaze.

"How are you feeling?" Ranger asked.

"Tired."

It was the truth. He couldn't remember the last time he'd felt that tired. That exhausted. That lost. He stared at his lap. Ranger's eyes were still pinned to him. He could tell Donnie was darting glances at him in the mirror too. They drove like that for miles, not speaking but observing Yates's fried mental state.

The usual anger bubbled up, the desire to growl and tell them not to look, but he let it build and pop. The anger seeped away, and he let loose another pent-up breath. He shifted forward, put one hand on Ranger's thigh, and his other hand on Donnie's shoulder. They both stiffened, but when Yates didn't dig his finger into their flesh, they relaxed.

"I'm sorry."

Ranger clutched his hand, Donnie gripped his other. The reaction was immediate, and neither snatched their hands away. They kept hold of Yates, and Yates kept hold of them.

The curled-up wires in Yates's heart pulsed with electricity. These two ridiculous humans had come to save him. They didn't have to or need to, but they'd wanted to. Guilt built in Yates's gut, and he couldn't lift his gaze away from his knees.

"You're not nothing to me."

"We know." Ranger snorted.

Yates blinked and risked a look at him. "How do you know?"

Donnie snorted from the front seat. "You use your contacts to plan our hits down to the smallest detail."

Yates turned back to Ranger, who nodded.

"All we've got to do is turn up and pull the trigger. It's your way of making sure we're safe."

"Occasionally things go wrong," Donnie said from the front. "Like Ranger getting shot during a burglary."

"And Donnie becoming a show-off and botching his hits."

Elliot banged his chest, near blinding Yates's with his smug smile. "And me, of course."

"But the point is"—Donnie sighed—"we know you care, and we care about you too. Hence us saving your arse today. We love you, man."

Ranger squeezed his hand. His watering eyes made Yates's sting. Even Donnie sniffled from the front. They shared meaningful looks, passing them around, letting them sink deep. He might not have had Dylan's love, but he had these idiots, and that was enough. It was more than enough.

"Love you too."

Elliot had twisted in his seat and gaped for the second time, and for the second time, a piece of gum dropped from his mouth into the footwell.

"What?" Yates growled.

Elliot grinned, flashing his pearly white teeth. "This might be the gayest thing I've ever seen."

Chapter Fifteen

Yates messaged Dylan and told him not to call, or text, or come near the shop. Then he blocked him. He threw up a barrier between them, a threat to keep Dylan away. Of course, he didn't listen. Dylan came to the house and banged on the door, calling for Yates through the letterbox.

He said he was sorry. Yates screwed up his face. The apology made it worse. It told Yates Dylan was aware he was hurting and knew what he'd done to create that hurt. It gave Dylan power and kept him in control.

Yates set out to shatter his control.

He limped down from his bedroom as Dylan bellowed through the letterbox for the twentieth time. He'd been there all day. Yates was sure of it. The sun had set, and the sky had darkened. Yates had been curious whether Dylan would've stayed there all through the night, but he scowled at himself for being curious. That meant he cared.

Dylan fell silent and stumbled back from the door. Yates unlocked all the bolts, took a deep breath, and swung it wide. Dylan attempted to squeeze into the house, but Yates caught him by the biceps and lifted him up. His cheeks were puffy and red, but Yates didn't look further than that. He didn't want to see Dylan's eyes.

He walked him back until they got to the pavement, then Yates set him down. Dylan wrapped his arms around Yates's middle and held him tight.

"I'm sorry, okay? I don't know—"

"It's fine."

Dylan panted. "What do you mean it's fine?"

"It's nothing." Yates gestured between them. "This was nothing."

"It wasn't nothing. Don't call it that."

"I don't want you to keep coming here anymore."

"Yates?"

"I mean it, Dylan. Don't come back."

Dylan licked his lips. They were puffy and raw too. "Let me explain."

"There's no need." Yates untangled himself from Dylan.

He looked over Dylan's head and shot a forced smile at Darius jogging across the road. It hurt his cheeks and didn't reach his eyes, but he kept it there, making sure Dylan saw it.

"Go straight in," Yates said.

Dylan froze and stared at Darius as he headed inside the house. He gripped onto the bottom of Yates's shirt and tugged it free of his jeans.

"Who's that?"

"Darius," Yates said.

Dylan threw his shirt away before clutching it tight again. He dropped his forehead to Yates's chest and spluttered into the material. "But I love you."

Motherfucker.

"No, you fucking don't," Yates growled. He cursed himself for growling, for letting Dylan's words affect him.

"I do. I'm sorry I went after Rick."

The name rattled in Yates's skull. He winced, pulling back, but Dylan kept a tight hold of his shirt, refusing to let go.

"Please, let me explain."

Dylan's pleas twinged in his chest. They sparked and uncurled the ragged parts of his heart. Yates couldn't allow it.

"Red."

Dylan frowned up at him. "What?"

Yates gave the hand scrunching his shirt a sharp look. "Red. It means stop, no questions, no hesitations. Stop."

Dylan released him.

"Don't come back here. Don't come to my shop either. We're done, Dylan, okay?"

Why the lift at the end, why the hint of a question? Yates hadn't wanted it, but yet it had forced its way from his mouth.

Turn and walk away. The order repeated in Yates's head, but his heart made him stutter.

"You'll be fine. You will be, Dylan."

Tears ran from Dylan's eyes. His bottom lip trembled. Yates thought of Eren in the mansion. He'd been fooled by the tears and the trembles and hadn't seen him as a danger.

Vulnerable men are the most dangerous.

Yates flexed his fingers, needing to stroke the tears from Dylan's face, but he didn't. He turned away and left Dylan on the pavement.

As soon as he closed the door, he sighed and dropped down the other side of it. Darius stood in front of him, suited, clutching a briefcase. His blond hair was in disarray after a stressful day in the office.

"What was so urgent?"

Yates snorted. "Nothing, it was all nothing."

"What?"

"Drink?" Yates asked, pushing off from the floor. He couldn't be that close to Dylan, couldn't hear his sobs or feel them in his chest.

"I'm driving."

"Just water then," Yates said, getting them both a glass of water. He watched Dylan out the window. He lingered like a lost puppy before leaving with his head down, tripping and stumbling from view.

"Yates?"

"What?" He spun around to face Darius.

"Did you not hear me?"

"Evidently not."

Darius thrust his fingers through his hair. "Look. Yates, I've got to tell you something."

"What?"

"I can't do this tonight." He gestured to himself, then Yates.

Yates blinked. "Right, yeah."

That wasn't the point of this. He'd invited Darius to drive Dylan away. It worked, mission complete.

"In fact, I can't do it any night."

Curiosity plucked at Yates, he frowned. "Why's that?"

"I've found someone."

"Found someone…"

"He is dominant and forceful. In the best kind of way." Darius sighed. "But he also kisses me like he cares, and holds me after, and does a load of other things I didn't even know I needed. I love him."

"Good for you," Yates snapped.

Darius sighed and moved away. Yates grabbed his hand to stop him.

"No, let me try that again." Yates smiled at Darius, and although tentative, he smiled back. "Good for you. You deserve to be happy and to find someone who makes you happy, not just abused."

Darius beamed, but the smile fell from his face. "Our sessions will have to stop."

They already had.

"Unless you're up for a threesome? That might work. He might be into that, as long as he's the one to cuddle me at the end."

"Thank you for the offer, but no."

Darius chuckled. "So, who's the kid outside?"

"He's nothing."

"Nothing?"

"That's what I said."

Darius looked away, a pondering expression flexed the lines of his forehead.

"Nothing is ever truly nothing, though, is it? It's one of those physiological things. There's always something. Always."

Yates rolled his eyes. "This is why we never sat down and talked."

Darius laughed again. Yates realized he'd never seen him laugh before, never seen him free and happy.

"What's your partner's name? And please God, don't say, Ranger."

Darius sucked in a breath. "I won't say it then."

Yates stiffened. "What?"

Another burst of pure happiness came from Darius. Smiles and joy looked alien on his face. Yes, he had messy hair and the same bags under his eyes from work, but he looked healthier somehow, almost excited as he shared his lover's name. "He's called Heston."

Yates snorted and raised his drink. "To you and Heston."

Darius clinked their glasses together, grinning like the happiest guy in the goddamn world.

Yates sagged when he remembered what it was like to feel like that.

****

"I told you to water them, not drown them."

Ranger sighed. "Never satisfied. I was either going to water them too little or too much; I chose the latter."

His flower shop resembled a jungle, with unpruned stems, leaves branching out toward the ceiling and soil everywhere.

"Don't worry, the roses are good."

Yates looked for them. "Where are they?"

"I picked off all the petals and sprinkled them over my bed for my date later."

"Ranger."

The name rumbling in Yates's throat felt almost pleasurable. It felt normal.

"Relax, they're in the office, safe and sound."

"They'd better be or else you're going through the window."

Ranger grinned. "Want to know how else I know you care about me?"

Yates pinched the bridge of his nose. "Stop replaying that moment in the car. Please, pretend it didn't happen. I do."

"I know because even though you threaten to throw me through a window every time I see you, you never have."

Yates gestured him out of the shop. "Don't push it. Today might be your day."

Ranger stepped out and slid his sunglasses on. "Nah, you've got somewhere to be."

Yes, he had.

"Do you know how else I know you care about me?"

Yates sighed as he locked the door to the flower shop. "How?"

"You told me you cared."

"Yes, we've been through this. I was overtired, and I'd been stabbed with a screwdriver."

"That wasn't the time I meant."

"When then?"

"When I was in the hospital."

Yates crushed the shop keys in his grip. "I didn't visit."

"You didn't visit with Donnie." Ranger gave him a small, almost shy smile. "But I know you did visit."

"How?"

Ranger flicked his ear. "I heard you. You told me to hang on, to keep fighting. To get better."

"You...heard me?"

"Yes."

Yates fidgeted with the keys, unsure what to say. Thankfully Ranger took the initiative. "You know that guy who stuck you with the screwdriver?"

"What about him?"

Ranger nudged Yates's ribs. "You could say he *screwed* you. Screwed you good."

"You're an idiot."

Ranger burst out laughing while patting Yates on the back. He folded his arms and glared, but movement on the other side of the road stole his attention. A car door slammed, and a woman jogged over and narrowly avoiding being knocked down. She stuck her middle finger up at the car beeping her.

Hannah.

She came to a stop in front of Yates, vibrating with rage. "Did you know?"

Ranger backed away with his hands up. "Later, bitches."

Hannah whirled on him. "What the hell did you just call me?"

"Nothing." Ranger reddened and darted up the street laughing maniacally.

"Answer me!" Hannah's sharp nail dug into Yates's chest. "Did you know?"

"Yes. I knew."

"You knew he was fooling around with my fiancé and didn't think to tell me?"

Yates sighed and turned around to unlock the shop. Hannah elbowed her way past and spun around to face Yates, wagging her claw of a nail.

"You were all in on it."

"I wasn't in on it. I was there for Dylan. I knew he'd been fooling around with Rick, but Dylan said they'd stopped, it was over."

"That doesn't make it all right."

Hannah rubbed her hand down her face.

"Of course, it doesn't."

"They were always too close. Me and Rick used to joke about it. Dylan had some crush on him, some daddy complex. It was completely one-sided. I thought once he went to university, it would stop. I thought he'd find someone else. I never for one second thought…" Tears swelled in her eyes. "I never thought they'd hurt me like that. Never. Five years. We were together for five years. When did it start?"

"I'm not the person you should be asking."

"Dylan said it happened when Rick started giving him rides to university, but what if it's a lie? What if it was happening at home? What if the whole five years they've been laughing at me behind my back, fucking in my bed?" She jabbed her forefinger into her temple. "See, I'm replaying everything, every moment between them, seeing more. Dylan's beams and his blushes."

"You need to speak to Dylan about this, not me."

Hannah pulled back her top lip. "I don't want to speak to him. I can't even look at him, knowing…"

She slapped her hand to her mouth.

Yates sighed. "Please don't vomit in my shop."

"What were you?" Hannah asked through her fingers. "Some decoy, some fake boyfriend to throw me off the scent?"

"No, I was just the idiot who fell for your brother."

Her anger cleared. "Did you see Dylan run after him?"

Yates swallowed. "I saw. It hurt more than I thought anyone could hurt me."

And he'd been not only petrol bombed but attacked with a screwdriver too.

"Then we're both better off without him."

Hannah's phone buzzed. She whipped it out of her bag and thrust it to her ear. "Stop calling me. When are you going to listen? I don't want to talk to you. I don't want to see you. When I think of all I gave up for you, to look after you, it makes me hate you even more."

Hannah's words tore a flapping hole in Yates's stomach. He clutched it, surprised he didn't see blood or his guts tumbling out. He swayed and clutched onto the display table as the past threatened to overwhelm him.

"You are dead to me, do you hear me? I'll be better off without you. I'd be better off with you dead and gone."

Hannah ended the call and yanked the door open. The bell didn't even have time to sound. Yates had grabbed the top of the door and forced it to shut. She yelped, spinning around.

"Yates?"

"Was that Dylan or Rick?"

He already knew, but her trembling bottom lip and the threat of tears confirmed it had been Dylan.

"Call him back, tell him you don't mean that."

"But I do."

"You don't."

Hannah smashed her fist into the door. "I do! I wish he was dead."

Yates recognized her anger, flushing her cheeks and stinging her eyes. It gritted her teeth and twitched a vein in her temple. He recognized it, but Yates knew where it would lead. The barriers, the walls, and in the center, the loneliness and the guilt.

"Picture him in a hospital bed, pale and lifeless."

"What?"

She yanked the door, but Yates didn't let it go. He glared down at her until she couldn't look away. "Tubes and machines feeding his body after an overdose you know you pushed him to. Picture his final moments, how he must have cried as he pushed each pill past his lips, cried, and thought only of the last thing you said to him. You wished him dead. So he fulfils that wish. Except it's not a wish, it's anger and pain and not knowing how to handle it."

Tears spilled from Hannah's eyes. She didn't speak but allowed him to bare his soul. If it helped her avoid the mistake he'd made, it would be worth it.

"Can you imagine replaying your words every day and imagining what his face looked like when you said them? How hopeless? How crushed? How his heart must've bled? Can you imagine arranging his funeral? Picking the flowers?" He gestured to the shop. "The flowers he loved but wouldn't get to see. Everyone offering you their condolences, but knowing it was you that put him in the ground."

Hannah looked away. "Can I not be angry?"

"Yes, be angry, hate him, but don't wish for his death, don't push him towards it. He's more vulnerable than you know, more confused, and hurt. It's so easy to look with only one perspective and not see it from the addict's point of view."

"Addict?"

"Yes, addict."

"Dylan hurt me."

"I'm not asking you to forgive him, I'm asking you to call him back and say you didn't mean what you said. I know you didn't. I can see it in your eyes." Yates wiped one of her tears away with his thumb. "You looked like me when I said the same words. I was angry that she'd gone back to drinking yet again, slurring down the phone, lying to me. I hated her for it. When the anger left, the realization caught up. I didn't mean what I'd said, but I didn't call my mother back to tell her that. I let my words hang. I let them torment her for days before she did as I asked."

Hannah lowered her head and stared at the phone still in her grip.

"I got the call to tell me what had happened while on tour. I got pity and compassion and was allowed personal leave. All the military operations I'd been involved in, yet that was what made me a monster. My words made me a killer. I turned her life-support off and watched her die."

The one murder he'd shed tears over.

"Trust me, you don't want to feel like that. You don't want to be heartless just to keep going. It's exhausting and unfulfilling. Life is fucking pointless. I think I live it only to feel this way for as long as I can as punishment."

Hannah pressed her thumb down on Dylan's name.

Yates released the door and backed off, giving Hannah the illusion of privacy.

She was quiet for a long time, then she spoke in a whisper. "I didn't mean what I said. I just…I'm…" Hannah shook her head. "I don't want to do this over the phone. Can we meet? Bloomers."

Yates froze, and their eyes snapped together.

"Why can't you come here?" She lowered the phone. "Why have you banned him from the shop?"

"It's easier."

"Right." She frowned and put the phone back to his ear. "He said it's fine, come over and we'll talk."

She hung up and slipped the phone back into her bag.

"I never said it was fine."

"You said you fell for him."

Yates blinked at her. "Did I—"

"Yes, don't make out it was nothing."

Nothing.

She looked away. "I hate what he did. I hate how he hurt me and abused my trust, but that hate is on the surface, a hard, and prickly, and unforgiving place." She pressed her hand to her chest. "But inside, deep inside at the moment, but it's still there, I love my brother, and I want him to be happy."

"Did you not hear anything I just said?"

"You said you're heartless."

"Exactly—"

The corner of her mouth lifted. "But you also said you fell for my brother."

Yates said nothing.

"Dylan couldn't keep his eyes off you the entire hen do. He looked happier when he looked at you, almost giddy. I've never seen him like that."

"You'd been drinking."

"And I saw you in the office, lost in your own world."

"I don't mean to burst your bubble and slap you round the face with this, but Dylan ran out of the ceremony room to be with Rick."

Hannah winced, Yates's guts pulled. They both grimaced.

"As you said, he's an addict, and he's never had the right treatment for it." She frowned, observing Yates. "You do know what happened after he ran after Rick, right?"

Yates turned away. "I don't want to know."

"I think you do…"

CHAPTER SIXTEEN

Yates's heart seized in his chest when Dylan passed by the window. He stopped in front of the door with his head bowed and knocked despite the sign being turned to open.

"Come in," Hannah yelled.

She'd perched on one of the display tables with Dylan's chair positioned in front of her in preparation for his interrogation. He pushed through the door, the bell rang out in cheer, and he winced. Tunnel vision led Dylan to the chair, and he sat down with his gaze locked on the floor.

His clothes were tatty, his hair had grown unruly, and when he lifted his head, Yates got a look at his downbeat expression. Sadness was etched on his face; even his freckles appeared dull. He looked like he did the first time Yates had seen him, when he'd asked to die.

Hannah's lips twitched. Yates recognized the anger flittering over her face, tugging at her features. She didn't voice it but pulled her gaze away from her brother and looked out of the window.

"What happened after you ran after *my* fiancé?"

Yates straightened at the possession in her tone, the bitterness she directed at the cars passing outside.

"I told you—"

"Tell me again."

Dylan snuck a look at Yates, then flinched at whatever he saw. Yates couldn't tell what expression he was pulling. His mind and heart were at war, and the battle raged across his features just like Hannah's. Anger and concern pitted against each other.

"I don't know why I ran after him." Dylan shook his head. "It was a knee-jerk reaction. I can't explain it. But it wasn't because I wanted him, I didn't want him, I don't—"

Hannah cut in. "Stick with what happened."

"I found Rick in the reception room. He said he couldn't go through with the wedding; his feelings had changed."

Hannah laughed bitterly.

"He kissed me."

Yates ground his teeth and flexed his arms. He tried to keep his expression neutral. One panicked glance from Dylan, and he knew he'd failed. He wanted to punch something.

"It felt wrong." Dylan took a deep breath. "I know it's a terrible thing to say, but it was the first time it felt really wrong. The first time my stomach churned, and I just wanted to get away from him. I pushed him away. I shouted at him."

"What did you shout?" Hannah asked.

"I don't remember. I think I yelled at him to leave."

"And what did he say?"

"He said no. He tried to kiss me again, but I pushed him away harder. I told him it would never happen again. Rick said how he knew I'd used Yates to make him jealous, to drive him crazy. He said it'd worked, and we should leave together. Get in his car and not look back." Dylan sniffled and glanced at Yates, then his sister. "I didn't want that."

"What did you want?" Hannah whispered.

"I wanted to keep my sister."

"You wanted to sweep it under the rug. Forget about it, not tell me the truth."

Dylan wiped his face. "Yeah, because I didn't want to lose you. Even if the guilt drove me mad, I didn't want you to hate me, and I knew you would. I knew you'd never forgive me. I begged him not to tell you, to leave, but he got angry and you came in, and he just blurted it out."

Hannah dropped down from the display table to her feet. "I didn't think I could feel any more hurt and humiliated, but then those words came from his mouth, 'Your brother and I have been having an affair.'"

"It ended months ago."

"He ended it."

Dylan scrunched up his face. "He did. I didn't end it. I knew I should've. I was angry that I didn't, but that didn't stop me messaging, asking him to meet, begging for a scrap of his attention."

Hannah trudged away. Yates thought she might leave, but instead, she stood in front of the door and shook her head.

"The more time I spent with Yates, the less I thought about him."

Yates huffed. "I'm the rebound then."

"No!" Dylan's eyebrows tugged together. "I stopped messaging, and it was him messaging and calling me. I didn't reply. I didn't pick up. When he came into the shop, his presence threw me off."

"You were awkward, more awkward than usual," Hannah said.

Yates was glad she'd picked up on it as well.

She hung her head. "Now I know why."

"I'm sorry."

"I'm sick of sorry. That word doesn't help. You robbed it of any meaning. Do you know what I want, Dylan?"

"What?"

"The truth. The ugly, disturbing, humiliating truth. I want you to tell me everything, going back over these five years—"

"It only started when I—"

Hannah spun around and pressed her finger to her lips. "I want to hear how you felt for the five years. I want to know at what point you fell in love with my fiancé, and I want to pick apart moments and see if he knew."

"Hannah—"

"That's what I want, Dylan. The only way I'll ever learn to trust you again is if you tell me the truth."

She looked at Yates and raised her eyebrows, darting her eyes towards the office door. He nodded and went inside, keeping the door open a crack to listen, but found himself too distracted.

Ranger had taken in the orders of roses, and they covered the office, drowning out the horrible scent and filling it with something greener. Something alive. Yates sat down in his chair and inspected the soft petals of the closest rose.

When had it ever been about the flowers?

He didn't know when it had happened.

Why of all businesses choose a flower shop? Ranger and Donnie had always wondered. They'd suspected it was some kind of joke. He didn't look like a man who liked flowers, and for the longest time, he hadn't, but she had.

His mother, an alcoholic. The woman who stole his childhood and years as a young man. Yates had liked to think of her as a villain, but it wasn't true. Addiction had been her villain, and sometimes she overcame it for a short while. Sometimes she saw the beauty in the world and him without thinking about the bottle. Those days, and weeks, and months, he'd been happy, but they'd never lasted.

Why flowers?

Drunk or sober, she loved them. Many times, he had to go in the morning and retrieve her from someone's garden. In her dazed state, she'd comment on the pretty flowers, always cheerful, always full of life. Other times she'd drive out and pay to see them, walk the ground of some snob's house and snap pictures to share with him.

He didn't care about flowers, but despite the last thing he'd said to her, he did care about her. Yates had hit his limit. He'd needed help and didn't know who to turn to, so he'd shouted instead, damning words that still haunted him every day.

Dylan appeared in the doorway, red-eyed and sniffling. "Hannah's gone. She said she needs space, then we'll build up the trust again."

"I'm glad you talked."

"She said she hates me, but she loves me too."

Yates snorted. He knew the feeling.

"Is that how you feel about me?"

"I don't hate you."

"You don't love me either."

"Dylan…"

He stepped into the room. "I wasn't choosing him over you."

Yates's nostrils flared as he replayed the moment at the wedding again. It hurt and made anger heat his veins.

"You ran after him."

"I don't even know why. When I was stood in front of him, I didn't understand why, and when he kissed me, I didn't want his mouth on mine. I wanted yours. I wanted you. I still want you. You make me feel calm and settled—"

"You do the complete opposite to me. You make me feel cornered and edgy."

"What? How can I? Look at me."

"It's not about size, or confidence, or experience. I respond to you differently, and I don't like it. I fucking hate it."

"You said you didn't hate me."

"And I don't, but I hate how I feel around you. Like I'm out of control, and the means I use to feel control, I can't use on you."

Dylan swallowed. An idea settled on his face. "You need to have control. That's why you have that arrangement with Darius."

The ended arrangement.

"Okay, I get it."

Yates frowned. *Did he?*

"You need to have those moments, those…meetings. It's a part of you. I can handle it… No." He shook his head. "I can't handle it, but I can accept it."

"What are you talking about?"

"I can share you with him."

Holy fuck. Yates bowed over like he'd been kicked in the stomach. "Share me with him?" He laughed.

Dylan didn't get it at all.

"I'm not gonna lie. I won't like it. I'll hate it. I died inside when I saw him go into your house. I couldn't sleep that night. I kept thinking about what you were doing with him. Darius can handle things I can't. I get it, but you can have that, and you can have me too. Please, Yates, give me another chance."

Yates surged to his feet. "Have you not learned anything?"

Dylan flung himself back against the wall, knocking roses all over the floor. He didn't apologize, and Yates found he didn't care about the flowers being trampled under his feet.

"You shouldn't share with anyone. Whoever you want should only want you in return, just you."

"But you said Darius gives you something I can't."

Yates growled. "I didn't say that at all."

He took hold of Dylan's hand and held it to his chest. It raced manically against his ribs, so swollen he could feel it pounding in his stomach and throat.

"You're a sadist. You get pleasure from giving out pain. I can't think of anything worse in the world than you hurting and humiliating me."

"I'd never do—"

"I want you, and I know I hurt you, but you still want me too. But you need that to be happy. You need a man like Darius."

"Don't tell me what makes *me* happy. Listen to me. Nothing happened with Darius and me that night. I invited him to the house purely so you'd leave. I don't miss my arrangement with Darius, but I do miss you."

"You miss me?"

"I don't crave hurting you. Dominating you, yes, but causing you actual harm? No fucking way. The thought of anyone hurting you makes me want to burn the world. The number of times I've thought about finding Rick…"

"Don't."

Yates flexed his jaw. "Scared I'd kill him?"

He sure as hell wanted to.

"Scared you'd get caught and sent away."

Dylan braced himself on Yates's shoulders and lifted onto his toes, but Yates swerved away from his kiss.

"But it hurt when you pulled away from me and went after Rick."

"I'm sorry."

Yates released a long breath. "I hate to sound like your sister, but I'm sick of sorrys. You broke my heart."

He inwardly cringed. It was like a line from one of the romance movies Ranger loved so much, but he'd felt it go twang in his chest.

"Let me mend it." Dylan gripped Yates's face. "Let me at least try, *please.*"

Dylan lifted himself up and ghosted his lips over Yates's, repeating the same word that chipped its way back into Yates's chest.

Please.

Dylan pressed their lips together, brief maddening kisses that lowered Yates's defenses each time their lips parted. *How could he do that?* How could he kiss so softly but break down a wall? How could this man, small and fragile in Yates's arms, smash a fist into his heart and lay claim to the tangled ruins inside?

Yates let himself crumble and kissed back. When they broke apart for air, Yates expected to see triumph, a gloating glint in Dylan's eyes, a self-assured curl on his lips. The way Yates looked when he broke someone down in the bedroom, but that wasn't the face staring back at him. Dylan's eyes had a glaze of emotions, his brow twitched, and his smile was so fucking relieved Yates's eyes stung at the sight of it.

This wasn't a game, or an arrangement, or a session. It was just them, as they were.

"I'm still angry," Yates said.

"I know."

"I don't know how to stop being angry. All I can see is you running after him."

"Don't think about it."

"It's not that easy."

"Why were you limping?"

He blinked. "Huh?"

Dylan didn't move from Yates's arms, but he looked down. "When you walked into the office, I saw you limping."

"I got attacked by a guy with a screwdriver."

"What?"

"A few new scars, nothing to worry about."

He pushed Yates away. A feeble effort, Yates released him anyway.

"Show me."

"Show you?"

Dylan nodded. "Take your clothes off. All of them."

"Really?"

"Yes, really. I want to see."

Yates sighed and unbuttoned his dandelion shirt. Dylan stepped closer and rushed it down Yates's shoulders.

"Easy."

Dylan gaped at the scabs down his bicep. "What the fuck happened?"

He didn't wait for Yates to answer. Dylan batted Yates's hands out of the way and undid his jeans. He shoved them down, and Yates climbed out, resting most of his weight on his good leg and not the other, which was blotched with purple and had two misleadingly small holes. It didn't look bad, but shooting pain accompanied his every step.

Dylan noticed his awkward stance and applied pressure to Yates's chest. He sat down on his chair and let Dylan inspect his wounds.

"You said you'd be fine."

"And I was."

Dylan poked his leg. "This doesn't look fine."

"I miscalculated a small detail."

The dangers of vulnerable-looking men.

"Come here." Yates pulled Dylan closer.

"What if one day you're not so lucky?"

Yates hummed. "I've been thinking about that, and maybe this"—he gestured to the roses around him—"is what I want."

"Flowers."

"The shop. My shop. I'll still plan Ranger's and Donnie's hits down to the final detail, but I'll retire from active duty."

"You can just do that?"

Yates smiled. "I'm an ex-assassin who prefers to run a flower shop. I'm an ex-sadist who's gone soft for someone."

He cringed. That hadn't come out how he'd meant it, but Dylan blushed and patted Yates's lap. "Not completely soft, but a little softer around the edges."

"You don't feel very soft."

"My point is what people want and need changes all the time, and what I want and need right now is you."

"Me?"

"But I swear to God, if you break my heart again, I'll kill you."

Dylan nodded. "Deal."

"Right now, I need and want you out of these clothes." Yates tugged at Dylan's T-shirt. "I'm starting to feel self-conscious sat here in my boxers baring all my scars and tattoos."

Dylan hooked his fingers under the bottom of his T-shirt, and Yates helped pull it over his head.

"You don't need to be self-conscious."

It was easy for Dylan to say with his blemish-free skin, soft as silk as Yates ran his weathered knuckles against his stomach. Dylan stroked his face, not shying away from his rough skin.

"You've never been afraid of me." Yates murmured.

"Not until I thought you wouldn't take me back."

Yates tilted his head and brushed his scarred eyebrow into Dylan's palm. "Why didn't I scare you?"

"I walked in on you jerking off to a meadow. How pathetic is that?"

Yates blinked, and blushed, and growled into Dylan's chest. "Little shit."

"Yates?"

"Yes?"

"Tell me what you want to do to me?"

Yates ground his teeth together, still riding a wave of anger. "I want to fuck you."

Dylan swallowed. "Fuck me?"

"Yeah. In the mouth, and then in your arse."

"Hard?"

"As hard as you'll allow."

Dylan looked away. "I've practiced hard."

"What do you mean?"

"With the annihilator. I've imagined it was you. I…I want it hard."

Yates squeezed himself. "Get on your knees, and I'll give it to you."

****

Yates clutched onto Dylan's hair, getting a good hold of him to force his head up and down. Dylan didn't shy away at the roughness. He moaned the more Yates tightened his hold and made his head bob up and down in time with his thrusts. He listened out and leaned back as far as he could to see Dylan's face, but there were no protests, only flushed cheeks and dark eyes.

He hit the peak, and rather than save himself or ease Dylan off while getting control of himself, he moved his hips harder, fucking himself to completion in Dylan's mouth.

"Don't swallow it," he panted. "Don't spit either. Hold it."

Dylan dropped off Yates's cock and pressed his lips together firmly to keep the cum inside. He waited on his knees, looking up at Yates with big, awestruck eyes. Yates snorted and reached into the desk drawer for the bottle of lube he hadn't used in ages.

"Sit," he said, slapping his thigh.

Dylan surged up and went to straddle him, but Yates had had second thoughts. "The other way, so you're facing away from me."

Dylan did as he was told, still holding a mouthful of come. Yates squirted a generous amount of lube onto his fingers before reaching between Dylan's legs, bypassing his drooling cock. It leaked all over the side of Yates's arm as he got Dylan ready.

"You okay?" Yates asked into his neck.

Dylan nodded.

"Move a bit so I can put it in."

Dylan leaned forward and allowed Yates to adjust. His lashes fluttered when Dylan's body finally accepted him inside. He took hold of Dylan's shoulder and leaned him back, letting gravity do the rest.

"If I'm too rough, spit it out and tell me to stop." Yates nipped Dylan's neck, and he squirmed. "But if you're okay with it, don't swallow my cum until I tell you."

Yates moved his hips. The chair whined, but he didn't stop. He pounded Dylan's hole until he was a fidgeting, sweating mess, brushing his cock back and forth over Dylan's prostate. Yates craned his neck, seeing as much of the side of Dylan's face as he could. A few times, he hit the right spot inside Dylan and his lips parted with a gasp, leaking cum out of the corner of his mouth. When it dripped to his chin, Yates let out a possessive growl and used his thumb to smear it over Dylan's lips. Rick wouldn't be kissing them again. No one would, except him.

Yates snorted and leaned into his chair to watch Dylan's back. He deleted the memory of him rushing after Rick in favor of the back of him, covered in sweat, riding Yates's cock. The longer strands on his head flapped as Yates fucked him, wafting strawberries and sweat to his seeking nose.

Yates wrapped his arm around Dylan, snaking his hand higher to get to his throat. He held on to him while plunging his cock into the heat of Dylan's body. He was close to coming again, a few more brutal thrusts, and he'd be there.

"Swallow me," Yates said, flexing his fingers on Dylan's throat. He felt the shift, Dylan taking his cum down just as Yates orgasmed and sent it shooting up.

Yates shuddered, loving that Dylan could feel him everywhere.

Dylan panted for breath, spent without coming. Yates took advantage of his exhaustion and grabbed onto his cock. He cried out, squirming on Yates's lap.

The sides of their sweaty faces rubbed together. Yates tried his best to pour out compliments while rubbing Dylan up and down. His still-hard cock was resting in just the right place inside Dylan, pressing on his prostate and making him leak in steady streams. Dylan whimpered for him to speed up with his hand and finished with a long lash of cum that splattered on the office floor.

He slumped on Yates's lap, completely shattered.

Dylan tipped his head back and whispered by Yates's ear, "I love you."

It was sappy, and cliché, and so ridiculous, but it spread a tingling warmth through Yates's whole body. Awed, he felt it most in his chest, the strings still broken but able to weave themselves back together into something stronger.

Yates eased himself from Dylan and turned him around. He rested his chin on Yates's shoulder and sighed as Yates drew shapes on his back with his fingers.

"It's a good job Tuesday at two isn't one of my peak times," Yates mumbled.

"Or it's a good job Fiona Florist is more popular…"

"Do you want me to send you through that door?"

Dylan leaned back. "Only if you'd go with me. I'd go anywhere with you."

"Then it's a good job I'm staying right here where you can study and fix your relationship with your sister."

Dylan bit his lip. "Say it, even if it's just once, say it."

"Say what?"

"You know what."

Yates gritted his teeth and flared his nostrils. He knew the words Dylan wanted. The same ones that had sent waves of warmth through his skin and swelled his chest. It was pathetic, so pathetic, but they hurt to say. They put barbs in his mouth and crushed his chest.

Dylan watched him with half-hooded eyes, smiling softly. Not insecure over Yates not being able to blurt them out. He waited, stroking his hand along Yates's damaged arm. *Damn vulnerable-looking men.*

"I love you."

The unease was worth the happiness glowing on Dylan's face.

EPILOGUE

The tubes and beeping machines were second worst to the frail body attached to them. Yates had seen such a sight twice already. His mother and Ranger. One lived and one died. Edna would be the latter. Her family had decided to switch off her life-support and let her go, and Yates could no longer avoid saying goodbye.

It was happening, whether he visited her or not, it would happen, and he wanted to speak to her like he had with his mother and Ranger.

He'd apologized to his mother, and he'd pleaded with Ranger.

But Edna?

Yates leaned over and whispered by her ear, "I killed him."

She didn't react. Yates had sat with his mother and Ranger enough times to know she wouldn't, but he hoped his words seeped into the last dregs of her consciousness. Yates had killed Mr Stevenson just like she'd asked him to.

"Tell me about her."

Yates straightened and looked over at Dylan sitting in the chair.

"Edna Green. Seventy-years old. Three children, two grandchildren. She lived on Maple Avenue with her cat Mr Big, who's now being looked after by her granddaughter, Sandy. She did Yoga on Mondays, Bingo on Fridays, and had her weekly grocery shopping delivered on Saturday afternoons."

Dylan stood up and patted the chair for Yates to sit down. He did, and Dylan sat down on his lap, gazing up at him with questions in his eyes.

"Tell me about her, about the her you knew."

Yates spoke loud enough for Dylan and Edna both to hear. "She started coming into the shop. Would spend ages looking at the flowers but never had a happy look on her face. She looked at the flowers with anger and sadness. It drove me mad."

"It doesn't take much," Dylan muttered.

Yates ignored him. "She came in every day, spent thirty minutes grimacing and sneering at my flowers, then she would leave. I snapped at her and told her if she hated them so much she should leave and never come back."

"Then what happened?"

"She wasn't intimidated by me in the slightest."

Dylan pressed a noisy kiss to Yates's cheek. "Because you're not intimidating."

"Then she told me about the flowers. She told me Rose had pigtails, and when she screamed, her voice faded. Open-mouthed screams with no noise. Daisy tried to get away, but they punished her for it. Iris cried about her mum and dad the longest. Poppy patched them up. Violet died in front of them." Yates's gut twisted. Dylan leaned away, wide-eyed. "They were all taken, including Edna here, and renamed after flowers, pretty flowers to be abused."

He pointed at Edna. "She was sold and abused until she got too old. She swore revenge, gathered evidence, did all this stuff to hunt Mr Stevenson, the ringleader, down, but she didn't want to live just for hate. She made herself a life, a husband, children, grandchildren, and her plans for revenge faded into the background until she got too old and too sick for her to fulfil them."

"That's where you came in?"

"Yes. She told me why she hated the flowers in my shop, but most of all the yellow lilies I sold. They'd changed her name to Lily. Flowers only reminded her of the bad, and I understood why she hated them, but I told her the lilies I sold were special. They were tiger lilies. Strong and fierce for as long as they lived."

Yates chuckled and looked at Edna. "I'll be straight with you, I had no idea what I was saying about them, but it brought a spark back to your eyes. You smiled this cruel smile at those lilies, then turned to me and asked me to kill Mr Stevenson, and I promised I would. I said I'd even suffocate him like a tiger. You liked that. You smiled again." Yates sighed. "I'm sorry it took this long to get him."

Edna didn't react. Yates hadn't expected her to.

"We became friends, and she'd ask about me and my life, and I don't know why but I'd tell her." He squeezed Dylan. "I told her about you."

"What did you tell her?"

Yates laughed. "That I gave you an annihilator."

"You did what?"

Dylan darted looks between Yates and Edna, growing redder by the second. "What…what did she say to that?"

"I should fuck you because life's too short."

Yates could feel the heat radiating from Dylan's face.

"She didn't want you to see her not at her best"—he looked over at Edna in the bed—"but this is better than him seeing you flying from a cannon."

Yates boomed a laugh, jogging Dylan on his lap. Dylan roamed his hands over Yates's face.

"What are you doing?"

"Checking you're not ill or something."

"Why do you think I'm ill?"

Dylan glared at him. "You just mentioned launching Edna from a cannon."

"It was her idea."

"I'm starting to see why you liked her."

He sighed, his heart stuttered, and he lowered his head. "That's how *I* knew Edna."

They sat with Edna until visiting time was over, then Dylan laced his fingers through Yates's and walked with him out of the hospital.

"Well, this is fucking unfair!"

Yates lifted his head and found Ranger glaring at them. Ranger jabbed his finger out at the source of his annoyance, their linked hands.

"Mr I-don't-want-a-boyfriend finds himself a boyfriend. It's unfair."

"I wasn't looking. It just happened."

"That's what Donnie said too, stupid advice. Don't look, and Mr Right and perfect and oh so handsome will just walk into you."

"Why are you at the hospital?" Yates asked.

"Right." Ranger revealed his other hand. "Dislocated a few knuckles."

Dylan hissed at the tight purple balloon of Ranger's hand.

Yates took a step closer to inspect it. "How?"

"Punched a guy on a date."

Yates raised his eyebrows. "You punched your date?"

"No, he was at the bar, smirking, and I got angry."

"You got angry?"

Yates sucked in a breath. Ranger getting angry usually ended in dead people.

"I managed to keep control of myself, though. Hit him once, he hit me. The fight was over."

"And I'm assuming he's still unconscious somewhere?"

"No, he took the punch to the face like a pro, then battered me in the ribs." Ranger clutched his side. "I'm waiting to see him come out of the hospital."

"Why?"

Ranger shrugged. "I don't know, but speak of the devil."

They turned and watched a man rippling with muscle leave the hospital. Yates tensed at the sight of him and squeezed Dylan's hand until he yelped.

"You broke his nose," Dylan whispered.

"Yeah, and he broke my ribs."

The man glared in their direction and made a harsh tutting sound with his tongue. A hoop piercing shone in his eyebrow, and his blood-splattered vest hung low over his smooth pecs.

"Oh, boy," Yates muttered.

"What? Do you know him?"

"No, but he's exactly your type."

Ranger frowned. "My type? I don't even have a type."

"The old Ranger did, and that over there is it."

The guy waited at the bus stop, glaring, posturing, making a slit throat motion. His muscles made Yates twinge with inferiority. The guy was easily as tall and wide as him and Ranger and staring like he wanted to run over and rip their heads off.

Yates tugged Dylan safely behind himself. "Let's get out of here. Ranger?"

Ranger watched the stranger with wide eyes and a dopey grin. If he were a dog, his tail would've been wagging so fast his arse would have lifted off the floor.

Jesus Christ.

"Ranger?"

His eyebrows twitched before lowering over his loved-up eyes. He sighed, blissful and at ease, then said with more certainty than Yates had ever heard him speak, "He's the one."

FLOWERSHOP ASSASSINS

Something tells me the path to Ranger's true love is going to be a bumpy one….I mean, I know because I wrote it, but still…

Special thanks to:
Lara and Alba for Beta reading.
Truus for naming Dylan.
Karen for editing.
Books&Moods for the amazing cover.
Danielle for helping me with those pesky mistakes.
And everyone who read So Pathetic! <3

If you enjoyed it, please think about leaving a review on amazon or goodreads and spreading the word on social media.
Even the smallest of reviews or a rating is a huge help in getting my books noticed <3

Are you on facebook? Why not come join the lockup for news, teasers, cover reveals etc. Louise's Lockup

If you enjoy The Flowershop Assassins, you might like some of my other titles:

Self-published titles:
Adrenaline Jake Series
The first in the novella series is free on amazon, and the second is free if you sign up to my mailing list: Sign up

Evernight tiles:
The Freshman
The Psychopath
The Rat
Balls for Breakfast
New Recruit
One for Sorrow
Two for Joy

Happy Reading
Louise <3

Printed in Great Britain
by Amazon